ROMANCIN...

Once enemies, the proud countries of Tamir and Montebello have come together to find Montebello's missing crown prince. Now Tamir's second-born son steps into the role he was born for and goes in search of the missing Montebellan heir....

Sheik Hassan Kamal: The Tamiri prince will do his part to mend the rift between Tamir and Montebello and bring peace to his people. But he never expected duty to be so pleasurable… or so dangerous to his heart.

Elena "E.J." Rahman: The spirited CEO has fought hard to attain her position in a man's world. Now she must resist the one man who makes her feel all woman.

Yusef Rahman: Will Elena's father put his hatred for Tamir aside and take a chance on an alliance that might end years of strife?

Kitty: Elena's assistant is not about to let her boss—and friend—pass up a chance for true love.

El-Malak: The terrorist known only as the Ghost is one of the Brothers of Darkness's most dangerous—and most elusive—members.

Secret-Agent Sheik
LINDA WINSTEAD JONES

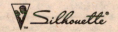

INTIMATE MOMENTS™

Published by Silhouette Books

America's Publisher of Contemporary Romance

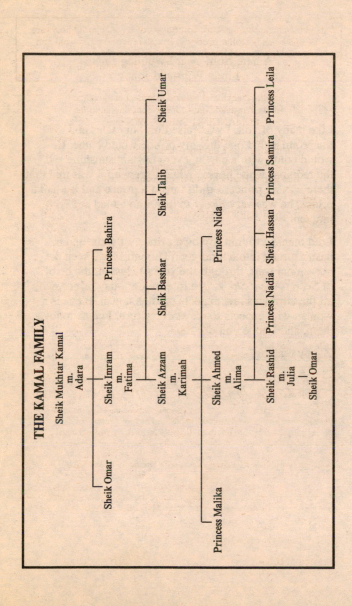

THE KAMAL FAMILY

Sheik Mukhtar Kamal
m.
Adara

- Sheik Omar
- Sheik Imram
  m.
  Fatima
  - Princess Bahira
  - Sheik Azzam
    m.
    Karimah
    - Sheik Basshar
      - Sheik Umar
      - Sheik Talib
  - Sheik Ahmed
    m.
    Alima
    - Princess Nida
    - Sheik Rashid
      m.
      Julia
      - Sheik Omar
      - Princess Nadia
      - Sheik Hassan
      - Princess Samira
      - Princess Leila
- Princess Malika

Prologue

Hassan hurried down the corridor toward the study that adjoined his parents' chambers. The thud of his heavy work boots on ancient tile resounded off the walls. His shadow, cast by soft lamplight that lined the hallway, followed him, dancing over the colorful mosaic that depicted the opulent palace lifestyle of another time.

He had been summoned, and because he had spent the afternoon at the refinery on Jawhar, the southernmost island of Tamir, it had been several hours since his father had sent for him. Their meetings were usually tense enough, without Ahmed Kamal's agitation being heightened by his having to wait.

As Hassan approached, the guard at the massive engraved door of Sheik Ahmed's study opened it for him, nodding silently as Hassan stepped inside. Ahmed Kamal was seated at his long mahogany desk, imposing and impatient as always. Hassan's mother, Alima Kamal, sat in her favorite place, a padded chair by the arched window that looked out

be true. Baraka Asad's family also has useful connections," he said insistently, "and for all I know she has a lovely laugh."

Hassan's own laughter held no humor. "How will we ever know? I don't think she laughs at all. Or speaks. Look at her the wrong way and I'm quite sure she'll faint dead away."

"Tahirah Boulus..."

"Has a nose longer than yours," Hassan interrupted, annoyed that his father's urgent summons was about this tired old subject. They'd had this conversation before, and it always ended badly. On this subject, as well as many others, they would never agree. "I have no desire to marry, Father. And if I ever do succumb to the temptation, I will not choose a bride based on her family's political connections."

"It is your obligation."

Hassan shook his head and pushed back his mussed hair with both hands. "Women have their place." In his bed, though since his mother was present he would not offer that assertion aloud. "If I ever meet one who does not bore me after a day or two, perhaps I will consider marriage." He doubted such a woman existed. While he adored women— their beauty, the softness of their skin beneath his hands, the warmth of their gentle smiles—he could not imagine spending his life with just one.

The old sheik slapped his hand on the desk. "I never should have allowed you to attend university in America! Those years made you insolent."

Hassan's mother cleared her throat, and both men turned their eyes to her. She did not lift her own eyes from the embroidery in her lap. "I feel obligated to remind you, Ahmed, that Hassan was insolent at the age of three, long before he went to university."

inside the Montebellan Palace, not our own, but we cannot rule out the possibility that the traitor is among us. Until we find the culprit we can trust no one.''

Hassan nodded. Whatever his father asked of him, he would do. The fact that the old man had actually admitted aloud that he trusted his second-born, often disobedient son, was enough. But Hassan had other reasons for taking on this task.

If his mission strengthened Tamir's ties with the West, all the better. And if he could do something to end what tension remained with Montebello once and for all, he would have made a true and important contribution to the welfare of his country. Recovering the missing prince, alive and unharmed, would heal a lot of old wounds.

Montebello and Tamir, countries that had been at odds for Hassan's lifetime and more, now shared a common enemy. Their determination to destroy the Brothers brought them together in a way nothing else could.

''I want you to infiltrate the oil refinery,'' Ahmed continued, ''under the guise of a possible merger. Your interests in the business, and in the American refinery methods, are well-known. Your defiance of me is also common knowledge,'' he added with a short-lived wry smile. ''No one will suspect your motives to be anything less than sincere, since you have recently made it clear that you wish to own and operate your own refinery.''

Rashid tossed a large envelope at Hassan. It slid across the desk until Hassan stopped it with the palm of his hand. ''The company is owned by Yusuf Rahman, but the actual operation of the refinery is left to his CEO, an E. J. Rahman.''

''A family member?''

Rashid answered, ''I would imagine, yes. We could not

Hassan lifted his eyes to study his father's stoic face. "The Ghost?"

Rashid leaned over to study the photograph himself. "They call him the Ghost because he has been fortunate or skilled enough to elude almost certain capture more than once, when the authorities closed in on the Brothers in Maloun. Makes more sense if we assume that he doesn't spend all his time in his home country, but actually lives in America. *El-Malak* is the only name we have, and that is the only photograph known to have been taken of him. He is most surely in charge of the American faction of the Brothers. You will find more details on his past included in the information you have been given."

The old man's nose twitched. "It is not much, I'm afraid."

"My appointment with the CEO is Tuesday afternoon," Hassan said, returning the photograph to the envelope. "When do I leave?"

"You will fly out tonight," Rashid answered. "Arrangements have been made. We will talk before you leave, concerning communications."

Hassan stood, more than ready to return to his suite of rooms in the royal apartments to look over the information needed to get started.

His father rose, too. There had been a time when Hassan and Rashid both had to crane their necks to gaze up at their imposing father, their little hearts full of love and fear and respect. Today it was the old sheik who had to look up at his sons, but the love and respect, and sometimes a trace of the fear, the children had for their father remained. They did not speak of the emotions and ties of their family, but even in times of conflict the feelings were there.

"Inside the envelope there are also intelligence photographs of other known members of the Brothers of Dark-

Chapter 1

Elena stood at the tall window in her office and glanced down into the parking lot. Sheik Hassan Kamal arrived right on time, whipping a black Ferrari into the parking lot two minutes before their meeting was set to begin. He took long, arrogant strides through the parking lot. His traditional costume—*gutra*, long jacket and baggy pants, all stark white—whipped around him as he made his way toward the building entrance with what could only be called impatience in his step. He glanced toward the refinery, less than half a mile away and clearly visible from the office building, but his gaze did not linger there.

Kitty slipped into the room, escaping from her desk in the outer office. "You look very pretty," she said primly.

Elena turned from the window and smiled at her assistant and friend. "I'm not supposed to look *pretty*," she said. "I'm supposed to look professional." Since she usually spent more time at the refinery than in the office, on most days she wore coveralls and work boots, and ended the day

potential partnership with the royal family of Tamir was more important than her own impatience with slackers. She could and would keep her opinions to herself, no matter how annoying the playboy sheik turned out to be.

The elevator on her floor pinged as the door opened, and at that moment the phone on her desk rang. Kitty walked across the room to answer the phone, and Elena proceeded into the outer office to greet the sheik.

He stepped from the hallway into the office with the same arrogance that had carried him through the parking lot. For a moment Elena was speechless. Kamal was tall, a good six foot two, and broad in the shoulders. He looked bigger face to face than he had from her window view. She tried to tell herself it was the traditional costume that made him seem imposing. If not that, then it was the touch of gold in the black braided silk that held his white *gutra* in place, the massiveness of the emerald on his right hand, the gold watch on his left wrist. But she couldn't fool herself. Beneath his loose, traditional clothing, this man was powerfully built. Strong and hard. The power that emanated from him had nothing to do with what he wore.

Even with sunglasses hiding his eyes from her, she could tell that he had an unusually handsome, olive-toned face. The cut of his jaw was sharp and masculine, the nose perfectly straight and fittingly regal, and the mouth...a mouth that sensuous should be illegal!

"Welcome to Rahman Oil," she said, recovering quickly and stepping forward, offering her hand for a crisp, businesslike handshake. The sheik took her hand in his, grasped it firmly, and brought it to his lips. She was so shocked when he touched her knuckles with that illegal mouth of his that she jumped. A tingle shimmied up her arm to her neck. The sheik wore a small, completely wicked smile as he re-

moved back and lifted her hand to indicate the open door, just as Kitty walked out and laid widening eyes on the sheik.

Kamal stepped into the inner office, and Elena turned to Kitty to request coffee for two. An obviously impressed Kitty mouthed "hubba-hubba," before heading for the coffeemaker and the full pot that awaited their visitor.

Hassan sat facing Elena Rahman. They were separated by a desk, two cups of terrible, weak coffee, and several unorganized piles of paperwork. He was still astounded that Rahman Oil's CEO was a woman! And an amazingly beautiful one, at that. Such a woman should have better, more appropriate pursuits to fill her time. He could think of a few, sitting here watching her as she told him all about Rahman Oil and the operations of their refinery.

She did seem to be knowledgeable, he would give her that. They had been discussing the refinery for over an hour, and she had answered every one of his questions without referring to notes or calling on an assistant. The CEO of Rahman Oil was not a mere figurehead—she knew what she was doing.

Surely Elena Rahman was not involved with the Brothers of Darkness. Not only was it unlikely that the Brothers would allow a woman into their organization, he was certain that he saw honesty and sincerity in Elena's green eyes. She was open, direct and earnest, and she had no qualms about looking him squarely in the eye. The longer he watched and listened to her, the more convinced he was of her integrity.

He set the certainty of her innocence aside. Appearances could be deceiving, and anything...anything was possible.

But Elena Rahman truly was beautiful. Her dark brown hair, sleek and straight, was cut short. The ends touched her chin and swayed when she moved quickly. Her seemingly honest eyes were a magnificent shade of green, and topped

he said, pushing the weak coffee the secretary had prepared aside. In truth, it didn't matter that Elena Rahman was beautiful, that when he had first seen her something inside him had clenched and fluttered, or that for a few wonderful moments he had forgotten the purpose of his visit.

"How about tomorrow morning?" Elena pushed back a strand of hair that brushed her cheek. "I have phone calls to make this afternoon, and I'm sure you must be tired, after traveling all this way. I'll make arrangements to have the proper safety equipment here in the morning. I hope you don't mind setting aside your traditional attire for the tour. The long loose fabric can be dangerous in a working plant. Steel-toed boots and a hard hat will be required, and I'm afraid I don't allow loose clothing on the plant. It's too dangerous."

"Of course," he said. He had worn the traditional attire thinking that if E. J. Rahman were a conservative Malounian he might be suitably impressed. All his suppositions about E. J. Rahman had been very, very wrong. He had done his best, but he suspected Elena was not at all impressed.

"Dress casually, and I'll have a pair of coveralls here for you to wear."

He nodded in agreement.

"Wonderful. Meet me here, and after you change I'll drive you out to the refinery." Elena stood, signaling that the meeting was over, and Hassan rose slowly to his feet.

The last thing he wanted to do was return to his suite at the hotel and try to sleep. Yes, it had been a long trip, but his mind was spinning. There was so much to be done, so little time. And yet, to push for an immediate tour of the refinery might seem strange.

Elena opened the door and gave him a smile as she tried to usher him out of her office. As he passed very close by the Rahman Oil CEO, Hassan sensed an uneasiness in her,

he let his mouth linger, just a moment longer than was proper. She shivered tellingly and he felt her response through his hands, through his lips.

This assignment might not be such a sacrifice after all.

Elena waited until Hassan's Ferrari left the parking lot at warp speed. "You're fired," she whispered without turning to look at the short, gleeful woman who stood behind her.

"I am not," Kitty said. "No one else knows the filing system. You'd be lost without me."

She *would* be lost without Kitty, but not because of Kitty's filing system or her efficiency as an assistant. They both knew Kitty's job was secure, even when she pulled stunts like this one.

"You couldn't just leave well enough alone."

Kitty snorted. "You didn't have any meeting tonight. You never did! A drool-worthy man asks you on a date, and you blow him off with a nonexistent business meeting? What's wrong with you?"

"It's not a date," Elena argued, something in her stomach flipping over at the very idea. "It's business. Just business."

"Ha." Kitty snorted. "The way that hunky sheik was looking at you, I could tell the only business on his mind was monkey business."

"If you think he's such a hunk, then why don't *you* meet him for dinner?"

Elena turned around in time to see Kitty wrinkle her nose. "I'm old enough to be his...well, not his mother, but I'm definitely old enough to be his much older sister, or an aunt or something. Besides, he didn't stare at me like he wanted to eat me up."

Elena's heart lurched. She had caught glimpses of that stare herself.

mother. Elena suspected he had loved her too much, and even something so simple as talking to his daughter about the woman he had lost was more than he could bear.

The knowledge that love could be so powerful scared her. Loving and losing Johnny had almost destroyed her. Maybe that was one of the reasons she had kept men and love at bay for so long. She was in control at all times. If a love like that were ever to grip her again, would she still be in control?

Her father had tried, more than once, to introduce her to men he thought suitable. Those he presented were all sons of Malounian friends or the friends themselves, older men Yusuf Rahman thought would make fitting husbands. He expected Elena to deny her American mother, to forget that she had been born and raised right here in Texas, and become a proper Malounian woman.

She had never been able to make her father understand that it was too late. After her mother's death, he had left her care to a series of nannies and then sent her away to school as soon as she was old enough. She could never understand how he could expect her to become the kind of traditional daughter he wanted her to be.

Old-world men, like her father and Sheik Hassan Kamal, had little time for an independent woman. Dinner was going to be a disaster.

"Wear the red dress," Kitty said, her smile drifting back.

"I don't think so."

"But you look fabulous in the red dress!" Kitty argued.

"I don't want to look fabulous," Elena argued.

"Yes, you do," Kitty said as she turned to return to her desk.

"Don't."

"Do!" Kitty said as she left the office.

tween Tamir and Montebello were healing. But there was still a long way to go.

Seeing nothing suspicious, Hassan shifted his focus to the office building that sat approximately a half mile to the north of the refinery. His gaze raked up the three-story building to the top floor, where he easily found Elena Rahman's window. He smiled, remembering their meeting. He had never meet a woman like her, of that he was certain. It was more than her unusual position that piqued his interest, more than her beauty. She was a fascinating woman, her eyes full of sweet secrets and tantalizing promise one moment, hard and strictly business the next. He could not wait to get her away from the office.

Yes, this was a job. A mission. He had to find out what Elena knew, had to use her to get to the information he needed. But when that was done....

As he moved the binoculars down, he caught sight of movement in the parking lot, and refocused his attention there. A man in a rumpled suit, he realized with disappointment, making his way to his car at the end of the work day.

But two women left shortly after the man. Elena and her secretary, talking animatedly, walked side by side across the parking lot. Hassan focused on Elena's face, watched her smile at something the secretary said, and then answer with a cavalier wave of her hand. He wished he could read lips. He wanted, so much, to know what she said. Was she talking about their dinner tonight? Or what might come after? She laughed, and her entire face lit up. Ah, that was not the face of a woman who was talking about oil, or the refining process, or the mundane details involved in the business side of Rahman Oil.

When Elena got into her vehicle—a red pickup truck, of all things—and drove off, Hassan lowered his binoculars. Their dinner wasn't until eight. He had plenty of time to

Chapter 2

Kitty had made reservations at the most extravagant restaurant in the area, darn her hide. Leon's was expensive, but
Elena had never heard anyone complain. The food was always excellent, the music soft and soothing, the lighting
romantically dim. And besides, everyone loved Leon. Even
on a Tuesday night, the place was bound to be crowded.

Elena left her truck with the valet and headed toward the
front entrance, her heart in her throat. If there had been any
diplomatic way to get out of this dinner, she would have
found it. She approached the entrance to Leon's as she
would the doorway to any other business meeting. Determined to be as tough as any man. Knowing that she had to
work twice as hard as everyone else to prove that she was
worthy of her place at Rahman Oil.

The door swung open as she reached it, and she stepped
inside, glancing up at the man who had opened the door for
her. She was completely unprepared for the sight of Hassan
Kamal in an expensive black suit, his longish black hair

the work. It should be easy to maintain her distance from a man whose thinking was so antiquated.

And then he smashed her resolve with words that had nothing to do with business.

"I like the way you say my name," he said with a smile that was surely illegal in some countries. "You say it... differently."

"It's my Southern accent," she confessed. "I'm surprised you like it. My father hates my accent." It was a personal confession, one better left unsaid, and she realized it, too late.

"I adore your voice. It's very soft and...slow. Not too soft or too slow, but warm and welcoming."

He seemed sincere. Perhaps she had been hasty in putting him in the same category as her constantly disapproving father.

Heads turned as Hassan escorted her to their table. Of course heads turned. There weren't many men like this in Evangeline, Texas. Or anywhere else, she imagined. He seemed unaware of the stir he caused, or maybe he was accustomed to being the center of attention. He didn't even seem to notice the eyes that followed them across the room to a secluded table by the window that looked out over a rambling, overgrown garden.

The casual hairstyle Hassan wore suited him, Elena decided as he held her chair out for her. The long, black waves that touched his collar and brushed his cheek made him look like a pirate, or a warrior prince. She half expected to spot a gold loop dangling from one ear, or a hint of an exotic tattoo crawling up his neck from beneath his starched collar. She saw neither, of course, and dismissed her fanciful musings with a shake of her head.

Hassan Kamal liked her Southern accent, or so he said. He himself had almost no accent at all. If not for just a hint

"I ordered for you," he said. "I hope you don't mind."

He'd ordered for her? Of course she minded. It was an outrageously presumptuous action. "That depends on what you ordered."

"The broiled shrimp and pasta, steamed vegetables, a pitcher of water with lemon and the chocolate mousse for dessert."

She relaxed. All her favorites. "You talked to Kitty, didn't you?"

He nodded. "I called your office this afternoon, after you and your secretary..."

"Assistant," Elena interrupted.

"After you and your assistant left for the day," Hassan finished, perhaps just a little amused. "The woman who answered the phone was kind enough to give me your assistant's home phone number. I hope you don't mind."

How could she mind? It would be unreasonable to be irritated because a man went to the trouble to find out what she liked to eat. "Of course not." But she would have to have a word with Stephanie, who usually worked until seven and knew better than to give out Kitty's home phone number. At least she now knew that the sheik could be as charming on the phone as he was in person.

"Tamir," she said, anxious to change the subject. "Tell me about your home."

Hassan had arrived at the restaurant frustrated. The Rahman Oil Refinery business office had been too busy for him to sneak into after Elena's departure. People working late came and went with too much regularity for him to make his way unnoticed up to the third floor. He had been able to get a closer look at their security system, though. There were cameras posted at all entrances and exits, but he now knew their positions and they could be avoided.

Texas. The time flew by, and he only wanted more. More time, more laughter. More Elena.

No matter what, he could not forget why he was here. There was more at stake than his fascination with a beautiful woman. The world was full of beautiful women. He knew that well.

Dinner had been delicious, the conversation had been delightful, and now it was time to move on. He was not ready to let Elena go. Not yet.

"Dance with me," he said, rising to his feet and offering his hand. A combo had been playing for the past half hour, their music low and ordinary, softly unobtrusive. Since the first note, he had wanted to take Elena in his arms and dance with her. A few couples danced on the small dance floor, occasionally talking as they moved in time with the music.

Elena stared up at him and raised her finely shaped eyebrows. "Excuse me?"

"I asked..." Ah, he had not asked, he had commanded. It was a bad habit of his, or so his sisters told him. "Would you please dance with me, Elena Rahman?"

She laid her hand in his and stood. "Of course," she said sweetly. "But if you want to dance in Texas, you really must go to the Evangeline Ballroom."

"Why is that?" he asked as he led her to the dance floor. She walked close beside him, fitting well at his side.

"Because while this is very nice, it isn't at all Texan." At the edge of the polished floor, she turned to face him and lay her hand on his shoulder.

"Perhaps you will take me while I am here."

"Perhaps," she said, sounding uncertain as they began to move to the slow music. She kept her body away from his, moving stiffly, making sure there was a decent space between them. Her eyes remained on his chest, perhaps his chin. She definitely did not care to look him in the eye.

So Hassan pressed. "You said nothing about your family. I know your father owns the refinery. What about your mother?"

"She died when I was a baby," Elena said, her voice low.

"You were an only child?"

She nodded.

"How?" he asked. "How did she die?"

"Car accident," Elena said. "She just...lost control and ran off the road. I don't know anything about her, except for how she died. My father didn't like to talk about her, and I eventually learned not to ask. It hurts him too much to talk about her, so I don't know anything about her life. What she liked, what she didn't like, if she wanted more children." Her fingers rocked absently against him. "All I have is this one picture that I found in an old box of photos, years ago. I hid it, because I was afraid that if my father knew I had that picture he'd take it away."

Elena lifted her head and looked him in the eye, at last. "I'm sorry. I didn't mean for the conversation to turn maudlin. I'm tired. It's been a long day." She tried a smile that didn't have its usual brilliance. "Maybe we should call it a night."

Hassan didn't want to let her go, but in truth he still had to check out her office before he could even think about going to bed. "If you wish."

He saw it again, that vulnerability Elena tried so hard to hide. She might be CEO of an oil refinery, she might be a modern, liberated woman. But she was also a woman who had secrets. A woman who needed a friend.

"Elena," he said gently, not stopping the dance just yet. "Is there a man in your life?"

Something on her face hardened, just slightly. "Why do you ask?"

* * *

There were five messages on her answering machine. All from Kitty. Each message said the same thing, in varying degrees of urgency. "Call me when you get in, no matter what time it is."

Elena kicked off her shoes and walked toward the kitchen with a smile on her face. Tired as she was, she knew she wouldn't be falling asleep anytime soon. A diet soda and a few pages of the book she'd been reading, maybe that would stop her head from spinning.

Hassan Kamal was everything she did not want in a man. Tamiri, for one, an old-world man like her father. Oh, he was of another generation, but he still had those archaic ideas about women, she was sure. He had been absolutely shocked to find that a woman was CEO. What on earth would he expect of a woman he was involved with?

Not only that, he was one of those demanding types. He didn't ask, he commanded. *Dinner tonight. Dance with me.* Another annoying trait of an old-fashioned man who expected his women to obey his every word. Heaven forbid that a female should have an opinion.

And he was too good-looking. Guys who looked like that were never easy to get along with. They were too accustomed to getting their way with a smile that made women's insides go topsy-turvy and their brains go to mush. Add to that fact that he was a sheik, a Tamiri prince, and you had a guy who was most definitely accustomed to getting his way. He had probably never heard the word "no."

So why did she like him anyway? Why was she actually considering seeing him again tomorrow night, and the night after that, and every night until he flew back to Tamir?

"Elena," she said to herself. "Looks like you're a sucker for a pretty face, after all." She shook her head in disgust. While she stood with her head in the refrigerator, the

Elena laughed. "Good night, Kitty." She hung up without waiting for another question from her nosy friend.

Almost immediately, the phone rang again. Frustrated, Elena picked up the receiver. "No," she snapped, "I did not bring the hunk home with me. No, he is not standing here with his hands all over me. Yes, I had a good time, but it wasn't the kind of *good time* you're thinking about. For God's sake, Kitty, if you think the man is that desperate and needy, *you* jump his bones."

She waited for Kitty's usual tart response, but all was silent. Someone, not Kitty, breathed. Her heart fell. Oh, no.

"I just wanted to make sure you got home all right," Hassan's deep voice crooned into the phone.

Elena closed her eyes and leaned against the wall. Stupid, stupid, stupid. "Yeah, thanks." Should she try to explain?

"I had a wonderful time tonight."

"Me, too." Until I embarrassed myself over the telephone...

"You are a very good dancer."

Bless him, he was going to ignore what she'd said when she'd answered the phone. "You, too." Her body relaxed, and she almost melted against the wall.

"And Elena," Hassan continued in a lowered voice. "I am not desperate *or* needy, but if you would like to...jump my bones, I'd be happy to cooperate."

Crap. "Kitty called a couple of times," Elena said softly. "When the phone rang I thought...it was just...I didn't mean..."

"Good night, Elena," Hassan said, saving her from her ramblings. Heavens, she could hear the smile in his voice. It lingered, even after he hung up the phone.

light off his waist and flicked it on. There were no cameras inside the building, not that he had seen on his earlier visit. In fact, security was incredibly lax. As one who had lived with some element of security all his life, he was appalled. The lack of guards, cameras, and an alarm system only strengthened his suspicions that Elena was not involved with the Brothers of Darkness.

But that didn't mean the information that Rahman Oil served as a front was wrong. And whether she was actively involved or not, there might be something in the CEO's office that would point him in the right direction.

He took the stairs, since he remembered seeing cameras in the elevators. He reached the third floor in no time, and stepped into the eerie hallway where Elena's office was located.

The door to her office was secured, and again he picked the lock without difficulty.

Rashid likely thought his little brother had no skills that might be considered useful for a spy. Little did he know that Hassan had discovered his propensity for analyzing how things worked early on in life, and had been picking locked doors around the palace since the age of eleven. An engineer who could not master a simple lock was a poor excuse for an engineer.

With moonlight streaming through the windows, Hassan no longer needed the flashlight. And with the windows uncovered, he ran the risk of being seen if he left it on. He switched off the light and hung it from his belt, while he went directly to Elena's private office. Once there, he sat in her chair and flicked on the computer. The screen came to life, along with a box for her password.

He cursed, and tried typing in a few words. *Rahman. Elena. Jumanah.* He smiled as he remembered the way she had enjoyed her dessert. *Chocolate.* All rejected. He sat

fact. It was only natural that Yusuf Rahman would want to hire immigrants from his home country.

Had Elena unwittingly hired men who were in league with the Brothers? How deep did their penetration go? It was impossible to tell from the innocent files in her computer.

He signed off and returned the photograph of Lydia Parker Rahman to the drawer, being careful to place it just as he had found it. As he did, he saw another small photograph stored in the back of that drawer. Hassan pulled it out, and when he turned this picture over his breath caught in his throat.

A very young Elena, her hair in a long ponytail and her smile wide, stood beside a young, fair-haired man who had his arm draped familiarly over her shoulder. Her arm was wrapped around the young man's waist. The man—no, the *boy*—in the photograph smiled with the same innocent joy that brightened Elena's face. They both wore T-shirts and jeans. The T-shirts were emblazoned with the words "Oklahoma State." Hassan flipped the photo over. On the back was scribbled, "Elena and Johnny, May 1992."

He returned the photo to the drawer, a little uneasy. For the first time he felt like an intruder. A thief.

But there was no time for recriminations. While he was here, he might as well check the other drawers in Elena's desk. There would probably be no need for him to break into the building again; he might as well make the best of this effort. In the bottom right hand drawer, Elena had stored feminine things. A small, soft bag of makeup, a brush for her hair, a spare pair of panty hose, still in the package.

The bottom left hand drawer contained more files. Schematics on the refinery, he saw as he leafed through. He rifled through the files, expecting to find nothing more.

The gun surprised him, lying there at the bottom of the

ran close by. "What's this?" he asked, pointing to an area that was under construction.

"We've had problems with the piping in this area," she explained. "My engineers are rerouting the conduit in hopes that will take care of it."

He looked over the duct carefully, walking around the area and finally climbing the ladder to get a closer look at the pipes that ran above their heads.

"What are you doing?" she called, hands on her hips as she craned her neck to watch him climb a good thirty feet. If he fell... "Get down here!" All she needed was a visitor to the plant falling and breaking his neck.

But Hassan climbed like a man who knew how to keep his balance and his footing. Of course he did. Hadn't she read somewhere that he'd climbed a mountain or something? Yeah. He'd climbed mountains, raced boats and dated supermodels. She had to remind herself that he was just a bored playboy looking for something new to play with. The new of the refinery, and of her, would wear off quickly. Of that she had no doubt.

"Just taking a closer look," he yelled, glancing down at her and flashing a quick grin. When he swung out to the side, holding on to the ladder with one hand and balancing on the sole of one boot, she held her breath.

His inspection completed, Hassan quickly descended the ladder. Elena was prepared to scold him for doing such a foolish thing, but he didn't give her a chance.

"You're using the wrong fittings," Hassan said as his feet touched the concrete floor. "They're not off by much, and I can see where your men wouldn't notice, but obviously they've been mismarked. And if you run the pipe around this way," he lifted his hand and gestured to the right, "your problem will be taken care of. You'll get a more natural flow that way."

"All right," she said. "Show me what you're talking about."

He did, quickly and effectively. Okay, so *now* she was impressed. Elena called Frank into the room, and once she showed him what Hassan had seen, he took the radio off his belt and called two other engineers to take a look.

Frank stepped into the outer room to wait for the other engineers, and Hassan turned to Elena and set his black eyes on her face. He looked like he was trying to stare through her. And succeeding.

"Leon's again tonight," he said lowly. "Eight o'clock."

"No," she said quickly.

Hassan raised his rakish eyebrows, but said nothing. She really should make an excuse. After all, Kitty wasn't here to contradict her, not today. And this guy was nothing but trouble. She could practically *smell* trouble on his skin.

She sighed in surrender. "While you're here, you really should see more of Evangeline than Leon's. I'll pick you up at your hotel at seven o'clock."

He grinned widely. "I look forward to it."

Unfortunately, so did she.

He followed Elena's directions, turning onto a two-lane side road. She had protested when he'd insisted on driving, but had quickly given in. He could see why she liked the pickup truck. It was a powerful vehicle.

As she had in her office today, before donning the black coveralls for their excursion to the refinery, she wore blue jeans and boots. The blue jeans she wore tonight were softer than those she had worn to the office. They molded to her legs in a most tantalizing way, as if they caressed her skin the way he longed to. The boots she wore this evening were low-slung leather cowboy boots that looked well-worn, rather than bulky steel-toed boots. Instead of a prim work

They followed the hostess across the room, and she tossed two menus on the table and told them the waitress would be by soon. As she left, she winked at Elena.

"She is a friend?" Hassan asked, leaning over the table.

"No," Elena said. "I just know her from the times I've eaten here."

"She seems very friendly."

"She is. Most of the people around here are."

Hassan reached for the menu, but Elena playfully snatched it out from under him.

"Uh-uh," she said with a smile. "Tonight *I* order for *you.*"

He settled back in his cushioned seat and crossed his arms over his chest. "Very untraditional," he said softly.

"Do you mind?"

He knew if he insisted, she would give him a menu and allow him to order for himself. "Not at all."

A waitress appeared and Elena, without so much as glancing at the menu, ordered two barbecue beef plates, tea, and chocolate pie.

Tea. Thank goodness. He hadn't had a decent cup of hot tea since arriving in Evangeline.

He had seen nothing today to make him think the Brothers of Darkness were active at the Rahman Oil Refinery, though that was far from conclusive. He'd only seen a portion of the plant. It was spread over more than a square mile, and he had only been inside a few of the buildings. There had been a large number of Arab faces at the refinery, but since he'd seen Elena's personnel files he'd expected that. Since the plant ran on twelve-hour shifts, four days on and four off alternating day shift to night shift, he had only seen one quarter of her people.

"Are many of your employees from Maloun?" he asked, forcing himself to remember why he was here.

"Both of them, to some extent," she admitted. She laid expressive green eyes on his face, and her expression turned serious. "But the real truth is, that refinery is all I've got."

"I find that hard to believe." Elena should have suitors he had to fight off to spend time with her, a family, an exciting life outside the mundane workings of the plant.

"Sad but true." She tried for a lighthearted tone, resting her arms on the table that stretched between them. "I don't want to talk about the refinery all night," she said, baldly changing the subject. "Tell me more about your sisters."

He saw that Elena was envious of his family, that she got some small pleasure from hearing him talk about his siblings and his parents. So he told her little stories about his sisters, small moments he had forgotten about until Elena revived the memories with her questions.

Their dinner arrived, and the waitress plopped two platters laden with food on the table, and then set huge glasses of tea beside the platters. Ice floated in the tea.

"It's not hot," he said needlessly.

"No it's not." She lifted her own glass and took a swallow.

He lifted his glass and followed her example, and almost spewed tea across the table. "And it's full of sugar!"

"Welcome to the South," she said as she placed her glass aside. "This is tea as it was meant to be. Cold, sweet, and strong."

He took another drink. Now that he knew what to expect, the iced tea wasn't so bad. In fact, it was very good.

"Delicious," he finally admitted. "Different, but I think I could get used to this. But while I'm here, I'm going to teach you to make proper Arabian coffee."

"You don't like Kitty's special blend?"

"No. It's much too weak. Have you ever had Arabian coffee?"

Chapter 4

Elena arrived at the office prepared to knock out a few mundane chores before Hassan arrived. He would stop by her office later in the day, since he had several errands to run this morning. He'd be searching for his Arabian coffee and pot, she imagined. She'd told him he'd probably have to drive to Galveston to do his shopping, but he hadn't seemed to mind. She'd expected that he'd simply call someone at the hotel and farm the chore out, but he'd seemed determined to find what he was looking for himself.

Hassan always surprised her. She'd expected a brainless playboy and found a mechanical engineer. She'd expected a macho jerk, and while he did have his moments, he was also a good listener and a fun date.

No, she amended with a shudder. *Not* a date. Their dinners together had been strictly business. So what if they hadn't talked business much at all, or if they'd ended the evening walking by the bay? He'd even taken her hand once, but that hadn't been at all romantically motivated.

Yusuf Rahman was a hard man. It was his nature, or so Elena told herself when she longed for a more tender, loving father. "Show him around the refinery, entertain him if you must. When all is said and done, if he makes an offer you will decline."

"But I think it might be good for the company..."

"I will not do business with the royal family of Tamir," he interrupted, all but snorting as he stepped away from her desk.

Her father frustrated her, and had for years. "Then why agree to the meeting in the first place? Why waste my time?"

He gave her a tight smile. "By the time I learned of the meeting, you had already accepted. To decline at that point would have been unwise. Humor the boy, be hospitable, but when all is said and done if he still wants to invest in the refinery, find something wrong with his offer." He patted her on the cheek as he passed. "You will think of a good reason to decline, I am sure."

Elena nodded, but she wasn't thinking of ways to get rid of Hassan, she was already thinking of arguments that might sway her father. If she could convince him that a partnership with Hassan would be good for Maloun as well as Rahman Oil, would he change his mind?

"Would you mind if I invite a few friends out to your ranch tonight?" he asked as he reached the doorway.

"Of course not," she said. "I only use it on the weekends, so no one will be there to disturb you." The ranch was a fairly new purchase, less than two years old and the result of the glaring knowledge that outside the business Elena had no life. Now she had a small ranch house an hour's drive from Evangeline, as well as three horses, and she employed an old couple that ran the place as they had for the people who'd owned the ranch before her. Since

"Monday morning," she said. "They'll be ready by nine."

He nodded absently, and ignored Kitty as he breezed out of the office, leaving a trail of cigarette smoke in his path. After the elevator in the hallway whished open and closed, Kitty stopped pounding on her keyboard and lifted a smiling face to Elena.

"So?"

"He wants to use the ranch..."

"No, no," Kitty interrupted. "Last night. Did you finally get lucky?"

"Kitty!" Elena used her best "boss" voice. "I'm sure you have better things to do than to quiz me about my love life." Or lack thereof.

"That's a no," Kitty said, shaking her head in despair as she returned to her keyboard.

Hassan leaned into the three-sided phone booth, trying to cut off the dull roar of mall noise surrounding him. The phone rang twice, before Rashid answered. It was 7:00 p.m. in Tamir, but Hassan's elder brother had been waiting for this call. Since cellphones were notoriously unsecure, Rashid had suggested they communicate by pay phone rather than depend on international cell transmissions.

"How are you?" Rashid asked, his voice low and obviously concerned.

"I'm fine," Hassan said. "I've seen the plant. I haven't found any concrete information yet, but there are a large number of Malounians employed at the refinery. I'll be there again this afternoon. Rashid," he added sharply, "E. J. Rahman is a *woman*."

There was a pause, a second or two of complete silence. "A woman?"

"Yes. What wonderful intelligence I was given."

her that in spite of everything, he wanted her in a way he had never wanted another woman.

It was the gun that stopped him, he supposed. The pistol in her desk drawer was out of character with the woman he thought he knew, an unpleasant surprise. No matter how much he wanted to, he could not absolutely rule out the possibility that Elena was somehow involved. In telling her why he was here he might put her, and himself, and the prince in mortal danger. Until he knew more, he could say nothing.

As Hassan flew out of the mall parking lot, his brother's words echoed in his head. *Don't try to be a hero.*

Again, Hassan surprised her. Yesterday he had taken an interest in the workings of the refinery. Today he took an interest in the people. With that charming smile on his face, he made an effort to speak to everyone. Not only that, he lent a hand whenever he could, and it soon became clear that he had participated in every job imaginable at a refinery. From production to maintenance to working the pumps at the dock, he handled everything like a pro.

Everyone liked Hassan, even if they obviously started out wanting not to. When he made it clear that he was willing to get his hands dirty, and that he didn't think himself too good to take on any job, they couldn't help but come around.

Her earlier presumption that Hassan wanted a piece of this refinery the way he might want a new toy he'd soon tire of had been as wrong as her other suppositions about the Tamiri prince.

They walked toward the cafeteria, an uninspired concrete block building that served good, plain food. It was too late for lunch, but since neither of them had stopped to eat a

spread his long legs, and watched her hard, in that intense way he had about him. A man in shapeless black coveralls shouldn't look this way, sexy and tempting and...gorgeous. Elena's heartbeat increased, her mouth went dry.

In all her life, she'd never met a man like this one. She'd never thought she would. He made her heart race with a glance, he surprised her, and he shared her passion for this dirty, difficult business. She tried to tell herself all that meant nothing. *Nothing.* He was a sheik, a prince, a member of a royal family. Eventually, he would return to the world he knew.

She worked for a living. The days were long, the pay excellent, but this was about as far from royalty as you could get. If he was a little bit fascinated with her, it was because in his world women didn't work for a living. And if they did, they certainly didn't dirty themselves doing a man's job. She was a novelty, nothing more.

When she turned back around, candy bar in hand, he grinned at her. It was the grin of a rogue, an easy smile that spoke of an easy life, a bucket of charm, and a way with women.

"You like your chocolate," he said.

"Every woman likes chocolate, pal," she said, forcing her heart back into a normal rhythm. Of course, the women outside Tamir that he knew well probably didn't eat at all. Models, she had read somewhere. Skinny, fat-lipped, fake-breasted models who probably didn't ingest anything but celery and bottled water.

"Not like you," he said, his smile fading as he walked toward her and the vending machine.

She skirted around him and sat at the table where he had left his drink and chips. She had few pleasures in life, and she wasn't about to let a man rob her of one by making her self-conscious.

and away from the most flammable tanks and the working area where a fire would be disastrous.

The fire brigade had not yet arrived, but it would take a few minutes for those specially trained men to leave their posts and gather their gear from the refinery fire station. They'd better hurry. Black smoke poured from the open door to the windowless shop.

Umair clapped one of the younger men, a maintenance worker named Donnie, on the shoulder.

"It happened really fast," Donnie said breathlessly, stopping to cough twice. "Chet was welding on a piece of pipe, and somehow he arced into the parts cleaner."

"He was welding near the solvent basin?" Umair shouted, his grip on Donnie tightening visibly.

"It was just a quick little weld," Donnie said, paling. "He said it wouldn't take any time at all. But he arced into the solvent. It flashed up, and I think it must've ignited some oily rags. Something blew and threw me to the floor. I must've been out for a minute, because when I came to the flames were pretty high." He shook his head and looked around. "Where is Chet?" he asked.

Umair glanced at the crowd that milled safely outside the machine shop, studying the faces there. "He didn't come out with you?"

The kid looked toward the shop. "The smoke was really black. I didn't see or hear him when I came to, so I figured he was already out."

Everyone stared at the smoky doorway. Black smoke billowed through, roiling up and into the once clear air. The fire brigade would be here soon. Soon enough for Chet?

Hassan turned to Elena, tossed her his hard hat, and spun back around before she had any idea what he was thinking. One minute he was studying the smoky doorway like the others who had gathered there, the next he was running into

As the fire brigade pulled their truck up to the building, Hassan emerged from the smoke with an unconscious Chet dangling from his shoulder. They were both covered with soot and Chet's clothing was badly singed. They were barely five feet from the doorway when the building was rocked with another explosion, this one strong enough to shake the building and send flames shooting from the doorway and toward the sky.

Trained paramedics saw to Chet, while Hassan brushed them off and ambled toward Elena with a tired grin on his face. A few of the men congratulated and thanked Hassan as he passed, a couple of them even patted him on the back, but he never took his eyes from her.

If anyone else had done such a foolishly brave thing, she'd start yelling now, at the top of her lungs. By the time she was finished, the culprit would find himself without a job. But three things stopped her. For one, she was so damned grateful that Hassan was unhurt that she couldn't possibly yell at him. Second, he had probably saved Chet's life. That second explosion had come too soon for the fire brigade.

The third reason surprised her, a little. She had never given much credence to the expectations of the Arab men who worked with and for her. This was not the old world, and they had better not expect her to act as if it were. But in that world, for a man to be publicly scolded by a woman would be considered disgraceful. A woman who dared to disagree was shameful, but to be publicly castigated...she wouldn't do that to Hassan.

"Are you all right?" she asked, trying to keep her voice calm.

"Fine," he said, his voice rough from the smoke he had inhaled.

She glanced down. "Your boots are singed."

"Of course not. No more worried than I would have been for any one of my men."

"Am I one of your men, Elena?" He trapped her against the truck, his hard body almost touching hers. She had never been more aware of his height, the width of his shoulders and the strength there.

Her heart kicked, her fingers itched to reach out and touch him. She didn't allow herself that luxury. "Hassan, this isn't..."

"Right, proper, a good time," he interrupted. "I know. But ever since I came out of that smoke-filled building and saw you standing there, I've wanted to do this." He lowered his face toward hers. His hand gripped her wrist, his too-near body kept her there, trapped against the door of the truck. "To be honest, I have wanted to do this for a much longer time, and I do not think I can wait any more."

Elena knew if she told him to knock it off, he would. All she had to do was whisper, "no," and he would back away before their lips ever touched. She said nothing.

She knew it was coming, she had known for days that this kiss was coming, and still the power of it took her breath away. Nothing touched, but Hassan's hand at her wrist and his mouth on hers, and still she felt the kiss everywhere. Inside, outside, all around. It was the kind of kiss that could change a woman, she suspected. Make her want more, make her expect...more.

Hassan's mouth moved over hers, the grip at her wrist loosened and his fingers began to rock there. Only vaguely did she realize that he tasted faintly of smoke. Her hand came up to rest on his waist. She needed that touch, to remain grounded while the kiss took her soaring.

Finally he took his mouth away, and when he did he sighed and laid his forehead against hers.

"Maybe we should forget about the picnic," she said,

Chapter 5

Kissing Elena had been a mistake, he'd known it an instant before his lips had met hers. Mistake or not, he couldn't have stopped at that point, any more than he could stop breathing.

When he'd stepped out of that burning building and seen her face, worried and angry and then obviously relieved, he'd known that he couldn't wait much longer to take the kiss he'd been thinking about for two days.

After the excitement at the refinery, the fire and the kiss, Elena had gone home and he'd returned to his hotel to shower and change clothes. But being apart did nothing to remove her from his mind.

Hassan believed in his heart that Elena was not involved with the Brothers of Darkness, but he had no proof. He was here to spy on her, to learn what he could about the Brothers and the location of the prince. If he got involved with her, if he found himself distracted by a beautiful woman and discovered nothing...no one would be surprised. His father

"You are still angry."

"Yes, I'm still angry," she said, sounding frustrated. "You could have died in there."

"Chet surely would have if I hadn't gone in."

The anger on her face faded. "I know, but..."

"You take good care of your people," he interrupted. He didn't think Elena would dare to admit that she cared for him, just a little, but if she did...he would be lost. This was tough enough as it was.

A heavily sedated Chet Rankin was sleeping, and a vigilant nurse refused to allow anyone into his room. Elena spoke to the family, a weepy mother and a white-faced father who sat in the waiting room, two brothers who paced. Elena didn't say hello and leave, she sat. She comforted. When the elder Rankin realized who Hassan was, that this was the man who had gone into the fire after his son, Hassan was subjected to an embarrassing display of gratitude. Mrs. Rankin even insisted on giving him a big hug, and promised to feed him a good Texas dinner once Chet was home.

When Hassan and Elena finally made their way back to the parking lot, the light of day was already dying. So much for their picnic. Instead of taking her home, Hassan drove a silent Elena to an almost deserted parking lot that looked over the bay. He parked beneath a streetlamp that came on moments after they pulled into the lot, and rolled down the windows.

"We should do this another time," Elena said, her eyes on the bay. "It's late, we're both tired." She sighed. "Maybe we should just call it a day."

Hassan reached into the narrow cab seat behind him and grabbed the cooler he had packed, placing it between him and Elena. He opened the cooler, handed Elena a bottle of water, and then folded the top back so she could see inside. "And throw all this away?" He grabbed two chilled glasses

allowed him to slip the mousse-filled spoon into her mouth. She closed her lips over the silver, and he slowly pulled the utensil from her lips.

"See?" he said as she closed her eyes and swallowed. "Not so bad."

"You're spoiling me," she said softly.

"Someone needs to," he countered.

Elena was tough, a woman doing a man's job. She was everything a proper Arab woman was not. And at the moment Hassan wanted nothing more than to feed her, wrap her in a soft blanket, and hold her close until she slept. He had a feeling it had been a long time since anyone had comforted her in any way.

"Why do you not have a man to feed you?" he asked, a little angry that she had given up so much for her business. For her business alone, or for the Brothers? He hated the indecision that slipped into his mind.

"You never have gotten over the fact that the CEO of Rahman Oil is a woman, have you?" she asked with a small smile.

"Don't change the subject." He fed her another spoonful of mousse. "We're not talking about business. Why aren't you married? You should have children, a husband..."

"You're beginning to sound like Kitty," Elena interrupted, her voice a bit too tight. "Many women choose career over family, these days. I know that's a foreign concept to you, but..."

"You need more than Rahman Oil to make you happy," he said gruffly. "I can see it in you, this yearning for so much more. A family. A life beyond the refinery."

Even in the fading light, he could see her blush. "If you must know, I was engaged once, a long time ago."

The man in the photograph, he assumed. Johnny. "What

She answered his kiss, gently drawing her breath in to taste him as he tasted her. Those fine lips trembled. Not with fear, he knew, but with a rapidly growing desire.

Hassan took his lips from Elena's and gave her a wicked grin he did not feel in his heart. "No more tears," he commanded.

"Yes, sir," she said, trying for a smile herself, a twist of her lips that was as heartfelt as his own.

"It's been a long day." He opened the cooler once again. "Chocolate, more chocolate, and then you need to get to bed." Alone, unfortunately.

A knock on the front door intruded on her sleep, and Elena rolled over and glanced at the clock. Five-thirty. Five-thirty in the morning! At first she was annoyed, and then she bolted up, coming wide awake. Something was wrong. Someone else was hurt. *Dead.*

She threw back the covers and jumped from the bed, her heart in her throat as she raked her fingers through her hair and raced toward the front door to the sounds of yet another soft knock. Hand on the doorknob, she looked through the peephole. And froze.

Hassan Kamal, wide awake and perfectly healthy, stood in the hallway.

The fear was replaced by shock. "What do you want?"

"I told you I would make you coffee this morning."

"At the office," she seethed.

"Is there a kitchen at the office?"

"No."

"I thought not."

"Just a minute." Elena turned around and walked slowly toward the bedroom. Her blue cotton pajamas were perfectly decent. She didn't have any nightwear that wasn't decent. But she'd feel vulnerable answering the door in her pj's,

same shades as the couch and chairs. Other than the plants and the candles, the place was fairly spartan. She didn't want or need a collection of knickknacks to dust. She'd spent many an evening alone in this room. Reading, watching TV. Not this week, though. This week she'd been too busy to crash on the couch all alone.

Hassan stopped studying the room and turned his eyes to her. Black, piercing eyes that seemed to house a thousand secrets. A thousand desires. Not quite awake, caught off guard, she couldn't help but think of yesterday's kisses. For the past eight years she had kept her distance, where men were concerned. The few social engagements she'd had since Johnny's death had been strictly business, and had ended with a handshake, not a kiss. She had forgotten how powerful a romantic kiss could be, how deep it could reach.

From the bedroom, the sound of her alarm interrupted her inappropriate musings. She spun around and presented her back to Hassan. "Kitchen's that way," she said, pointing toward the arched opening in the wall that led to the dining room. The large kitchen was just beyond. "Have at it. I'm going to take a shower and get dressed."

The coffee was boiling, the small porcelain cups he had purchased sat waiting on the counter of Elena's ultra modern kitchen. The shower had stopped, so Hassan hurried as he searched through the files on Elena's home computer. Fortunately she had used the same password here as she had at the office. That lapse had saved him a lot of time.

One of the three bedrooms had been converted to a home office. He hadn't had time to carefully study all the paper files, but in rifling through he had seen nothing but standard paperwork. On the computer, he discovered nothing but that Elena played a lot of FreeCell.

The low hum of Elena's hair dryer ceased. She would be

She ruined her coffee with milk and sugar. Lots of sugar. Leaning back against the counter, she closed her eyes, took another sip, and seemed to enjoy the strong brew.

"Better?" he asked.

"Much." Her eyes met his. "Are you hungry? I have lots of leftover chocolate cake and pie in the refrigerator."

He shook his head.

She smiled, a soft, reluctant grin. "I think I've actually had enough chocolate myself, for a while."

"Too much of a good thing?" he asked.

She shuddered, just a little. "Maybe."

Today he would once again search the refinery, using any excuse he could to work his way into the good graces and confidences of Elena's employees. Perhaps if he looked hard enough and long enough, someone would make a mistake and give themselves away.

"Tonight..." he began.

"I have work to do tonight," Elena interrupted tersely. "Really. Lots and lots of..." her eyes met his and she sighed. "Work."

She was afraid. Of the kiss, of losing control. He knew, because he shared her fears. "You mentioned the Evangeline Ballroom," he said. "You said I should go. Surely you would not make me venture into such an unknown place all alone."

At the end of the day, when he'd done everything he could do for his father and his country, he wanted to dance with Elena. He wouldn't be here much longer. Either he would find what he was looking for or he would be called home. Yes, he wanted to dance with her. He wanted to hold her and move in time with the music, and while they danced he would imagine all the things they would never do.

Elena shook her head and finished off her coffee. When she placed the cup on the counter, he saw the surrender in

"Investors are usually satisfied with a quick peek and then they're out of here," Umair said, no sign of his quick anger remaining. Visibly, he was calm once again. "You've been out here three days in a row, poking around. Makes me antsy, that's all."

Hassan grinned. "I have no designs on your job, if that's what you're worried about."

Umair shook his head. "Most days I'd gladly let you have it."

They walked toward the water treatment building, and Hassan glanced at the plant manager. "How long have you been in this country?" Umair's face was Arabic, but his speech and mannerisms were pure Texan.

"My folks came here when I was six," he explained, squinting against the bright sunlight. Before they reached the water treatment facility, Umair came to a sudden halt. "Can I be up-front with you, Mr. Kamal?"

"Of course."

Umair laid those black eyes on Hassan's face. The man was not intimidated by Hassan's position or wealth, and he wasn't as impressed as his men had been by yesterday's daring rescue. "I'm not worried about my job. I don't mind showing you around the refinery. However, if you plan on taking advantage of Elena in any way, I *do* mind."

The admonition chafed Hassan's pride, more than a little. "You are very protective of your employer."

"I've known Elena since she was a teenager," Umair said. "First as the owner's daughter, then as an employee. She started here as green as you please, but she learned quick and she knows the refinery business as thoroughly as any man you'll ever find."

"I have noticed that."

"If you think you can move in here and take advantage

a man came around the building. "I'm sorry," he said. "We're doing maintenance at the moment and the building is closed to visitors. Another day," he said. "Maybe next week."

"I might not be here next week," Hassan replied, taking a single step forward.

By this time there were half a dozen employees in the area. All water treatment employees, and all Malounian. Where was the racial mix he had seen elsewhere? Where were the friendly smiles?

Hassan offered a smile of his own. "All water treatment facilities are about the same, I imagine. Sorry to have disturbed your work." He waved casually and turned his back on the men. A tingle of warning crept down his spine as he walked away.

Hassan didn't look back, but he had a feeling all the employees at the water treatment building watched without moving from their posts. This was the first unusual incident, the first sign that Rashid's information might have been correct. There was nothing to be done at the moment, but he'd be back to see more of this area. Tonight.

white western-style shirt that was stark against the dark skin at his throat. Elena's eyes were continually drawn there, to the place where flesh met cotton.

They sat across the table from one another and sipped at large glasses of sweet iced tea. The noise in the Evangeline Ballroom, a huge building that looked like a warehouse on the outside and a barn with a polished floor on the inside, was almost deafening. The loud music, the laughter, the shouts of pure joy from the more exuberant dancers—Elena's ears were already ringing.

Hassan had put in another day at the refinery, helping out where he could and asking endless questions. When he'd arrived at her office, that first day, she'd expected nothing more than a perfunctory examination of the facility and perhaps one more business meeting to discuss financial matters. Instead he had come on like gangbusters, quickly making himself a part of the operation.

She had never expected that he would take an interest not only in the plant, but in the people who worked there. He asked questions about everyone, and this afternoon he had been very curious about Umair.

The Chicken ended, and the band struck up something softer, gentler. A good old-fashioned Texas waltz.

Hassan looked at her and grinned. "This I can do," he said, exiting the booth and offering his hand to her.

Elena placed her hand in his waiting palm and stood. Nothing had gone as planned this week. Nothing. A part of her wanted to shake her fanciful musings loose and force her life back into its regimented routine. Another, stronger, instinct she hadn't known was a part of her demanded that she close her eyes, drift along, and see what happened next. She had never, not once in her life, been tempted to go with the flow.

Hassan was a good dancer, she knew that well from their

not much, but I have a few horses, and there's a really great path along the river. Do you ride?''

He gave her a look that said, without a word, *Do I ride? Of course I do. I ride better than you. I ride better than any man.* He said all that with a lift of his eyebrows and a mischievous twinkle in his black eyes. "I would love to spend the day at your ranch."

"Good."

The music ended, the dance came to a close, and they stood on the dance floor awaiting the next song. Neither of them wanted to move, it seemed. They stood there, transfixed, caught between one song and the next.

But the band leader announced a twenty-minute break, and the spell was broken. Hassan took her arm and they made way for their table, walking arm in arm through the crowd.

"Elena?" She recognized that voice, and spun to face Cade Gallagher as he descended upon her with a widening smile and a question in his eyes. "What are you doing here?"

Before she had a chance to answer, he wrapped his arms around her and gave her a big hug, followed by a kiss on the cheek. "I don't think I've ever seen you here before."

When he released her, Elena stepped back and looked up at him. "You come here often?"

"When I'm in town." His eyes drifted past her to land on Hassan. The friendly look he had given her vanished.

"Cade this is Hassan," she said, keeping the introduction simple.

The men each extended a hand for what looked to be a not-so-friendly handshake. They stood almost eye to eye. Hassan was an inch or so taller, but Cade made up for the lack by being a tough as leather Texan who never backed down an inch. Cade and Hassan sized one another up as

"Good to see you," she said, reaching up to kiss him quickly on the cheek. "Call me sometime." She wouldn't hold her breath waiting for that call, though she did wish it would come.

When Cade sauntered off, Hassan took her arm and guided her toward their table. "Who was that?" he asked testily as they sat.

Elena smiled across the table. "The first man I ever loved," she answered. "My first summer romance."

Hassan's eyes narrowed. "Really?"

Elena smiled widely. "I was eleven and home for the summer, enjoying a vacation from boarding school. Cade was seventeen and already a heartbreaker. Every night I wrote about him in my diary."

"I would like to see this diary," Hassan said, visibly relaxing as he realized that her love had been that of a child.

"Sorry. I burned it years ago." She leaned across the table. "Some secrets should never be revealed." Her smile dimmed. "Actually, he's my brother."

"Your *brother?*"

"Adopted," she added. "His parents died when he was a teenager. First his father, and then a short while later his mother. Mrs. Gallagher and my father were friends. When she passed on, she named my father Cade's guardian."

"And now?" Hassan asked. "I haven't seen your *brother* at the refinery."

"Cade and Dad parted ways years ago, and not on good terms," Elena explained. "I swear, they butted heads at every turn. This all happened before I joined the business, so I wasn't there to smooth things over." Or to be privy to what caused that final rift.

"You do that, don't you?" Hassan asked with a smile.

"Do what?"

"Smooth things over for your father."

well. A slip of the tongue? Or did he not want her to know what he said?

She didn't ask him to translate. The words sounded tender and sweet, and at the moment that was all she needed.

Hassan parked the truck off the road, behind a grove of thickly leaved trees where it would not be seen from the refinery, should anyone look this way. It had been less than half an hour since he'd dropped Elena off at her condo, promising to pick her up at nine in the morning for the drive to her ranch. Eight hours from now.

Dressed in black and carrying bolt cutters he approached the refinery from the north, beside the railroad tracks. Finding a spot in the fence that was not well lit, he dropped to his haunches and began to cut at the base of the chain link and then up the side. He cut just enough to make an opening to squeeze his body through.

He slipped quietly through the opening, his body shielded by darkness and the railroad car between him and the refinery. Once he was on the other side, he repositioned the fence so it looked undamaged.

There was only so much he could see of the refinery, during the day. Asking to be shown an array of warehouses, examining the tanks themselves, would be suspicious. If he were hiding a prince, he'd choose one of those two places. An empty oil tank or a rarely used warehouse.

Or the water treatment plant, he thought as he moved silently toward the nearest tank. The all-Malounian crew and their determination to keep him away this afternoon were more than enough to raise his suspicions.

As he had entered on the north side of the fenced property, he started there by examining the tanks. He quickly found them unguarded and being used for their intended

closed door to the nearest pump room. When he was satisfied that no one was in the small room, he opened the door and searched it quickly, finding nothing unusual.

In the next room, a table and four chairs had been set among the pumps. Nothing else. Surprisingly, there was an ashtray filled with ashes and cigarette butts on the center of the table. No one smoked at a refinery! Not even here, where the air was dank and damp.

Hassan continued his search, uninterrupted. There was no sign of a more stringent guard below ground, no sign of the prince he searched for. He crossed a catwalk to the opposite side of the building, descended the stairs, and continued his search. When he found a locked door, his heart leaped into his throat.

This was a flimsier lock than the one on the outer door, and he had no problem getting past it with the tool he wore on his belt. The door swung open on a disassembled lab. No lights shone here, as they had elsewhere.

He was no spy, no trained investigator, but the hairs on the back of his neck stood up as he flicked on his flashlight and stepped into the lab, closing the door behind him. At the opposite end of small room, the beam from his flashlight arced across a wooden crate. Hassan dropped to his heels before the crate, and lifted the lid.

Guns. A crate full of Colt Commandos, a short barrelled version of the standard M16 rifle. There were not enough weapons here to supply an army, but there were definitely enough to arm a faction of terrorists. And who knew what other small rooms might house crates such as this one? He wouldn't have time to search them all. Not tonight.

But this crate was enough to confirm the suspicions that had triggered this mission. *El-Malak.* The Ghost. Somehow Hassan knew the man had been here. Rashid's information

from the opposite ground floor hallway. It was enough to stop him in his tracks and send him low, so that he lay belly down on the catwalk, looking through the metal grating to the floor below.

"When will we see some real action?" one man asked.

"Soon." The second man's voice was calmer, a notch lower.

The two men stepped into the dimly lit open area below, where they were surrounded by piping and working pumps.

"I did not come to America to work at a refinery." The first man, who had a harsher voice than the second, sounded frustrated.

Hassan wanted to see their faces. He had to see. Moving soundlessly, he shifted so he could see through the widest opening in the grating. One of the men put a cigarette in his mouth and struck a match. For an instant, Hassan saw their faces clearly. They were both Arab, probably Malounian. One was short, the other tall. These were not men he had met, but then he had not worked on this shift, and even if he had...apparently the water treatment facility had its own crew.

"You won't be here long," the smoking man said. "I have it on good authority that soon we will have a true battle to fight for our noble cause."

"Why do we wait?" the smaller man asked.

"Money," the smoking man growled. "We wait for money."

"Soldiers do not think of such mundane matters."

"Well, someone has to, unless you want to wage war with rocks."

They talked a few minutes longer, the tall man tossed his cigarette to the floor and stepped on the glowing butt, and they headed for the door.

Even after they had departed and no sound of their voices

Chapter 7

Buying the small ranch had been the best thing she'd ever done, of that Elena was certain. Her weekends here, getting away when things were running smoothly at the refinery, had added something special to her life. A touch of peace, perhaps. A life beyond Rahman Oil. Usually she stayed for the weekend, but since she'd invited Hassan she'd make it a day trip this time.

The ranch house itself wasn't much to look at. A rambling white-frame structure more than fifty years old, it always needed some kind of repairs. Wilson and May Carlton had run the ranch for the previous owner, and had agreed to stay on when Elena bought the place. Wilson took care of those repairs and the horses, and May kept the house clean and cooked whenever Elena or her father used the ranch house. They had their own smaller cottage beyond the stables.

Spring was a great time to come here, Elena thought with a smile as Hassan brought his truck to a stop. Flowers bloomed profusely around the long, deep front porch. On a

"Good morning, Wilson." Since the man was eyeing Hassan suspiciously, she introduced them.

Wilson, who stood better than a head shorter than Hassan, offered his hand, and the men exchanged a quick greeting. The older man quickly sized up the foreigner who stood so much taller than he did, and in his usual way found approval and offered a smile.

"Didn't know what time you'd be here," Wilson said as he stepped past them and headed around the stables. Out back, a corralled area gave the three horses Elena had acquired room to graze and run. A section of fence running down the middle separated the two geldings she'd had for a while from the stallion Wilson had recently acquired for her.

On seeing the horses, Hassan smiled. "Beautiful animals."

"Smokestack is mine," she said, stepping up on the bottom rail of the fence and pointing to the gray. "You can ride Buttermilk." The gentle gelding was named for his color.

Hassan glanced at her and raised his eyebrows. "You expect me to ride an animal named Buttermilk?" he teased.

"Unless you brought your own horse."

His eyes shifted to the black stallion in the separate corral. "What about that one?"

"Lightning," she said. "He's new, and no one's been able to ride him, yet. Wilson said he was spirited, but we're about to decide that he's a bit *too* spirited. Can't even get a saddle on him."

Hassan's intense gaze remained on the animal, the black stallion with the thin streak of white shooting down his nose. "You do not put a saddle on an animal like this one," he said softly. He stepped down the fence line, moving closer to the restless stallion.

"What on earth did you say to make him behave this way?" Elena asked, amazed.

"'When God created the horse, he said to the magnificent creature, "All the treasures of the earth lie between thine eyes,"'." Hassan continued to move steadily toward her. "'Thou shalt cast mine enemies between thy hooves, but thou shalt carry my friends on thy back. This shall be the seat from which prayers rise unto me. Thou shalt find happiness all over the earth, and thou shalt be favored above all other creatures, for to thee shall acrue the love of the master of the earth!'" Hassan reached her and stopped, perhaps a foot away. Perhaps less. The horse remained directly behind him. "'Thou shall fly without wings and conquer without sword.'"

"That's from the Koran," she said.

"Yes, it is."

"Listening to you talking to Lightning, I almost wish I had learned Arabic." And then she would have known what he'd whispered to her on the dance floor, last night. She didn't dare ask.

Hassan smiled. "Perhaps one day I can teach you."

It was a nice thought, but she knew Hassan wouldn't be here much longer. He definitely wouldn't be around long enough to teach her Arabic. Or anything else.

Elena raced her gray gelding across the countryside, her hair flying back from her face, her body perfectly relaxed and in tune with the animal beneath her. She had obviously been riding for years, perhaps all her life, as Hassan had. What a picture she made as her horse galloped along beside Lightning.

Hassan had to hold the stallion back. The beast within the horse wanted to break free, to run wild. And he had a feeling that when this beast ran, it flew like the wind.

Oil." Something on her face tensed, as if that memory was a painful one.

"The world is a big and wondrous place, Elena," he said, his voice low. "Sometimes we get caught up in one, small aspect of life to the exclusion of everything else. But that doesn't mean the rest of the world stops."

She grinned, and took the opportunity to change the subject. "You've seen a lot of this big and wondrous world, haven't you? You've traveled, done exciting things, been to exciting places."

"Yes."

"Evangeline, Texas, must be pretty tame, compared to some of the places you've been."

"I wouldn't say that." No, his time here had not been tame, and he had a feeling things were going to heat up considerably before he departed.

"After all that traveling, why did you decide to get back into the refinery business?" she asked, settling down to pick at her own sandwich. "It must be very dull, after the life you've led."

"What do you know about the life I've led?" he asked lightly.

"What I read," she confessed, eyes on her plate. "Mountain climbing, racing sailboats, dating unnaturally thin women with fake…assets."

"All true," he said.

"So why give that up to get into the refinery business? It's not like you need to earn a living."

He tried to turn the tables on her. "Why are you CEO of Rahman Oil? Your father has money. He could support you, or find you a husband who would support you, or…"

"Ack!" she said, tossing her sandwich aside. "This is the twenty-first century, Hassan. I don't need anyone to *support* me."

that kind of peace. It seemed he had been searching for something all his life. Perhaps this was it. His destiny. His home.

After watching for a few minutes he lay down beside Elena, casting his eyes over the water as she did. There was something mesmerizing about the sun sparkling on gently flowing water. There was a cadence to the nature here, a rhythm that slowed his heart and made everything but this moment seem insignificant.

Dappled sunlight covered them both, soft and eerie. The horses grazed nearby. Wildflowers in a dozen colors grew on the grassy hill and along the river bank. And Hassan kept his eyes on Elena, as he moved his face toward hers.

One quick kiss, that's all he needed. No, he thought as he descended upon her, he needed more. He needed everything. But for now, a single kiss would have to be enough.

Elena turned her head to meet his advance, closing her eyes as his mouth touched hers. Holding her breath as he kissed her gently. His heart pounded, his body responded quickly, and when the time for one quick kiss had come and gone, still he kissed her.

Elena's lips parted, her body shifted slightly toward his. Her hand, trembling and uncertain, rested against his side.

Lips parted and touching lightly, their tongues danced. Lightning coursed through his body. Had he thought one kiss would be enough? He wanted Elena with every fiber of his being, in deep, hidden places he had not known existed.

But he couldn't have her. Not now. Not yet. He took his mouth from hers, slowly, reluctantly, and she allowed him to back away. The light in her eyes almost drew him back in, but he resisted the urge and moved his gaze to the river again. Elena sighed and did the same.

associated with. She had a *brain,* and while her figure might not be eye-popping, it was real.

She made herself take a good, long look at the man whose kisses made her think ridiculous thoughts. He was a sheik, a prince of the royal family of Tamir. He took his pleasures with women from around the world, but when it came time to get serious…he would marry a Tamiri woman, someone who had been carefully chosen for him. She knew how that world worked, and there was no room for her in it.

She wasn't a proper Tamiri woman suited for a prince, and she didn't casually sleep around. That left no room for her in Hassan's life, nothing beyond the unexpected friendship they had found and forged.

While she contemplated this uncomfortable realization, the sky darkened. She turned toward the house and muttered a curse. A wall of black clouds approached, moving fast.

"We'd better get back," she said. Hassan followed her worried gaze, and agreed with a nod of his head.

They raced toward the stables and the house, but they were not fast enough to beat the rain. The storm met them halfway to the stables. Soft rain fell upon them, at first, then a stinging, harder rain that made them lower their heads. By the time they saw the waiting ranch house ahead, they were caught in a downpour.

Wilson waited for them at the stables. Elena and Hassan dismounted and handed over the reins.

"May left some stew in the slow cooker," Wilson said as he took charge of the horses. "And biscuits on the stove. All you have to do is pop them in the oven for ten or fifteen minutes and you'll be set."

"Thanks," Elena said, then she turned and ran toward the rear entrance to the house. She was already soaked to the skin, and still she ran. It shouldn't feel good to get caught in the downpour, but it did. Before she reached the

jeans, and an Oklahoma State T-shirt from the chest of drawers. She ran a comb through her tangled wet hair, and stepped back into the hallway. It was late afternoon, a time when there should have been plenty of sun to illuminate the house, but the clouds from the storm made the light dim. She flicked on the hallway light and knocked on the bathroom door. "Toss your wet clothes..." At that moment the light in the hallway went out, and the house was caught in a dead silence. No tick of the clock in the living room, no hum of the old refrigerator. "Into the hall," she finished softly.

The bathroom door opened and Hassan, wearing a towel wrapped around his waist and nothing else, stepped into the hallway. "The bathroom light went out."

"They all went out," she explained. She saw that he had hung his wet clothes over the shower curtain. That would have to do, for now. "It happens all the time, when it storms out this way."

"I'm sure the electricity will be restored soon," he said sensibly.

"Last time it took them twelve hours to get the power back on. We're kinda last priority." His bare chest was practically in her face. His long legs and bare feet were almost as distracting. "I have a robe I think will fit you," she said, spinning around and heading for her bedroom. He followed, staying close behind but stopping in her bedroom doorway and waiting there while she rummaged in the closet until she found what she was looking for.

"Here," she said, turning around with the garment clutched in her hand. "Wear this."

"No," Hassan said softly as she reached him.

Her eyes snapped up to his face. "No?"

"It's *pink*," he said, sounding truly horrified. "And there are ruffles."

Chapter 8

The rain came down so hard it seemed to pound on the roof with a vengeance. Thunder shook the little house, the flashes of lightning that accompanied the thunder lighting the room at irregular intervals.

Elena stood before the window and watched the lightning streak across the sky, hugging herself as she studied the storm. "I don't suppose we should try to drive in this," she said softly.

"No," Hassan agreed, watching her as intently as she watched the storm. He felt ridiculous, in a T-shirt that hugged his torso and the blanket he wore like a long skirt. Elena knew they could not leave the house in this storm, and yet she was obviously anxious to get away. The attraction they both felt simmered in the air, crackling like the lightning.

He had built a fire in the stone fireplace, and except for the occasional flashes of lightning that shot through the room, it was the low flame from the fire that provided the

Elena didn't have spare men's clothing laying about her ranch house. It didn't mean she had never brought a man here before, only that there was no special man in her life. "We haven't discussed merger plans in several days," he said, trying to sound businesslike in spite of his attire. "Perhaps this would be a good opportunity."

Elena seemed quite relieved to have a safe topic of conversation. "How involved would you want to be, as a partner?"

"Very," he said emphatically.

Even in the low light of the fire and the candle on the table at her side, he could see that Elena blushed. "I suspected as much, after watching you work the past few days. With that kind of involvement, you might want to...live here, at least part of the year."

"Most definitely."

"But..." she laid her eyes on his face. "Hassan, I have not been able to convince my father that having you as a partner would be a good idea. He's reluctant to trust anyone outside the family with anything as important as ownership, no matter how small the percentage might be."

It crossed Hassan's mind, briefly, that he could become family...

He shook the thought off. "Perhaps I should meet with your father. I can be very persuasive, you know."

"Maybe next week. As you can tell, he doesn't spend much time at the refinery, or in the office. He prefers to let me handle the day-to-day operations, but he does make regular appearances. He insists on having the final say in all major decisions, like this one."

"Who does the hiring?" he asked.

"We both do," she answered. "And some of the hiring is left to Umair."

Umair was Malounian, openly suspicious, and protective

there should be plenty of ice in the freezer. It hasn't had time to melt, yet."

Hassan shook his head. He did not want Elena to move. She looked too good, sitting there with the firelight on her face and the fear of something unknown sparkling in her eyes.

"Well, I'm parched," she said, jumping up quickly and leaving her rocking chair, padding across the main room of the house toward the kitchen. As she reached the end of the room, she snagged a candle and carried it with her.

Hassan couldn't help himself. He stood and followed her.

She had placed the single candle on the kitchen table, where they had shared a meal not so long ago. The candle cast just enough light for her to see what she was doing as she took a glass from the cupboard and ice from the freezer. When she saw him standing there, she assumed he had changed his mind and took down another glass. More ice. When she went to the pantry, where all was dark, he followed her, crossing the room on silent bare feet.

This was a terrible idea. He should have stayed in the living room, sitting on the couch twiddling his thumbs. The last thing he needed to do was to touch Elena. He wanted her too much. There was too much unresolved between them.

But one more kiss. Surely there would be no harm in something so simple and necessary.

She turned and stopped in the pantry doorway, a soft drink grasped in each hand, a look of surprise and anticipation on her face. Trying to appear calm and unaffected, Elena held one of the cans aloft. "Will this be all right? It's all I…" she held her breath as he took the two cans from her and reached just beyond her shoulder to place them on a shelf. "Have," she finished softly.

With his hand on her chin, Hassan forced Elena to lift

them aside. Maybe she did need to call a halt to this…but not yet. Not yet.

Hassan's hand raked up her side to cup one breast in his palm. The touch was gentler than the kiss, tentative. Did he think she would push him away? No. She couldn't, not even if she wanted to. A moment later a thumb rocked up and across her nipple, and she quivered in response.

Hassan's arousal pressed against her. There was no denying his response to this kiss. Elena knew she should remind herself of where she was, who she was, why she should call a stop to this here and now. But she didn't. Hassan was a luxury she would not have long, and she wanted to enjoy every moment, every kiss, every shudder. She had thought she would never shudder like this again…

While one hand caressed her breast, the other dropped from her hip to her thigh and traveled gradually upward until he touched her intimately, his fingers barely touching her through the thick denim of her jeans.

She was tempted to spread her thighs, take Hassan's face in her hands, and invite him into her bed. This feeling was too powerful to toss away, too wonderful to deny. But one realization stopped her. Hassan Kamal had the power to break her heart, a power no one else in this world possessed. She already loved him a little, she supposed. His smile lit up her heart, and she looked forward, with great anticipation, to every moment they spent together. She dreaded the day he would leave.

And he would leave. He might talk about buying into the refinery and making a home here, but whatever personal connection they had wouldn't last. Hassan thrived on excitement, and there was so little excitement to be had in her life. He wouldn't stay. He would break her heart. If she were a more modern woman she would be satisfied with the here and now. She would take the pleasure he offered and not

not happen. He sensed that there was something special between them, something he had never experienced before. If he took Elena now, if he claimed her in the way he so badly desired, what would she say when she found out the real purpose of this visit? And she would find out. He could not leave her behind, and when this was all over he could not continue the lie. She deserved the truth, no matter how painful it might be.

The sooner this mission was finished, the sooner they could get on with their lives. He wondered if there would be so much as a chance for that life, once Elena knew the truth.

Sleep eluded Hassan. No matter how complicated his life became, he could always sleep. Not tonight. His desire for Elena and his need to please his father and serve his country were at war, and in his heart he knew who had to win. He could not sacrifice the needs of his country for a woman. Not even for a woman like Elena.

He had been scheduled to call Rashid hours ago, but there was nothing to be done. The phones were out, and even if he had been bold enough to ask to borrow Elena's cell phone, she got no signal here so far from everything and everyone. Rashid would simply have to wait.

Frustrated, he threw back the sheet and stood. If he wasn't going to sleep, why lie here and torture himself? Elena spent time here. If she was involved in some way with the Brothers, however small, would there be a clue? Some tiny detail she had forgotten?

Hassan wrapped the blanket around his waist and knotted it at his hip, took the candle from the bedside table, and left the bedroom. He wanted to walk to the end of the hallway and open the door to Elena's bedroom, but he fought the urge and stepped from the hallway into the main room. His eyes raked over the room, coming to land on the desk in

der. "I don't like guns," she said softly, her smile completely gone.

He thought of the weapon in her drawer at work, but said nothing. How could he?

"I could have sworn I heard drawers opening and closing. Were you in the kitchen?"

Hassan's eyes looked over Elena's shoulder, and his heart dropped to his knees. The bottom drawer, the one he had been searching, was not completely closed. The candle on the desk lit that evidence clearly.

Elena began to turn.

"Yes," he said, stepping toward her. "I was in the kitchen. I thought you might have something that would help me sleep."

"Sleeping pills?" she asked, only hesitating in her rotation.

"Tea," he said quickly. "I thought I could heat some water over the fire and make some tea."

"The tea bags are in the pantry." A moment longer, a small rotation, and she would be looking directly at the desk and the telltale drawer.

Hassan reached Elena and laid stilling hands on her shoulders. No matter what, she could not turn around and look at that desk. "I don't think tea would do me any good," he confessed. "You keep me awake, Elena. *You.* How am I supposed to sleep when you lay so close to me? How can I rest when I know I can't have you?" The truth came easy at a time like this. "You wouldn't understand."

Her eyes were on him, her search of the room forgotten. "Of course I understand. Why do you think I can't sleep?"

He took the bat from her hand and propped it against the nearest chair. Elena shook her head and started to turn away once again. If she continued, she would see the partially opened drawer. She would know he had been snooping in

of being hurt. Not physically, but in her heart. The lies he'd told would hurt her; the truth, when she learned it, would hurt her.

"But the desire is stronger than the fear," she whispered. "I need you." She kissed him sweetly, briefly, her tender lips barely touching his, a caressing hand brushing against his bare chest. Her fingers trembled, her lips quivered. "Make love to me."

Hassan carried Elena to the rug before the fire, laid her there and hovered above her for a long moment. With an easy hand, he began to unfasten the buttons of her cotton nightgown. This was what she wanted, what he wanted as well, more than he'd ever wanted anything. It was right. The right woman, the right place. And yet...this was not the right time. There was too much left unsaid between them. Too many secrets.

What was left of his conscience fled when Elena reached down and unknotted the blanket at his waist, tossing back the ends and uncovering his nakedness. Her hands raked down his back to his hips, where they rested possessively, soft and yet strong.

He lowered his mouth to hers, but did not kiss her. "No matter what," he whispered, "tonight is for us, Elena. Nothing else matters, nothing but this."

She agreed with a nod of her head and an encouraging shift of the hands that held him, a telling shift of her hips as she unconsciously aligned herself to him.

"Just us," he said again, kissing her softly, quickly, then drawing away. "There's nothing of importance outside this room. Not tonight."

kissed the hollow of her throat, flicking his tongue there. Her body responded, as it did to all his kisses, with an almost violent intensity. The night air was cool on her bared breasts, but the shiver that worked through her body had nothing to do with the temperature of the room.

Hassan touched her, covered her breasts with his hands and ran his fingers over the gentle slope as if he had never caressed a woman before, as if he were learning her curves with the tips of his fingers. Elena closed her eyes and simply felt, savoring the sensation of his hands on her body, marveling in the desire that grew so rapidly within her. Her body throbbed, her bones quivered.

He lifted her into a sitting position, cradling her in his embrace as he slipped the nightgown down her arms. When her shoulders were bared he kissed her there, raking his lips across her skin while one hand worked the nightgown down. He undressed her that way, pushing her nightgown and panties down and off while he continued to hold and kiss her, to taste her flesh and arouse her until she felt like she was on the verge of shattering into a thousand tiny, fragile pieces. She was practically in his lap, their legs intertwined as they sat before the fire.

Elena still knew this was a bad idea, she still feared for her heart. But with that last kiss they had gone too far. There was no turning back, not now. She needed this the way she needed water and breath. She laid her hands on Hassan's face, cradling him in the palms of her hands. She looked him in the eye, feeling brave. Fearless.

"I have never wanted anything the way I want you," she confessed, wonder in her voice. "I've never felt this way."

"I'm glad," Hassan whispered. "I want to be the man who makes you feel in ways you have never felt before." He gently urged her back, until she lay on the rug and he hovered above her, his body long and hard and sheltering,

Hassan guided himself to her, pressed his erection against her waiting body and slowly pushed to enter. He moved almost languidly, never hurried, never beyond control. With each second that passed, he was deeper inside her. His body rocked, and she began to rock with him, urging him deeper, stretching and opening to take him into her body.

He took his mouth from hers and pushed his body up to look down at her as he began to withdraw and then surged forward to fill her completely. Firelight danced on his body and hers, and the wavering shadows made his face appear harsher than she remembered. And then, a moment later, softer. Sweeter.

He made love to her that way. Harsh and soft and sweet. It was beautiful. He was beautiful. The way his body fit hers was beautiful. As he stroked her, her world narrowed and there was nothing but the heightened stimulation of his body inside hers. She reached for him, with her body and her heart. She closed her eyes and rocked her hips against his, and when he drove deeper than before she shattered, climaxing with a soft cry that broke from her throat. She went over the edge, and Hassan came with her, plunging deep one last time and shuddering above and inside her.

He did not leave her, but lowered his head to her shoulder and rested there. She could not see his face as she threaded her fingers through his hair and found her breath once again.

It had been such a long time since she'd allowed a man to touch her. Such a very long time. Hassan had asked, why him? And she had no answer to that question. Long before they'd kissed, Hassan had touched her in a way no one had, since Johnny's death. He made her feel like a woman, he made her want more from life. And she could deny it all she wanted, but he did touch her guarded heart.

Unwanted, a tear slipped down her cheek. She didn't make a sound, but Hassan somehow sensed her distress and

and beautiful, she wished, so much, for there to be more. The realization was startling, since she had given up on *more* long ago.

A warm blanket covered them both, as they sat before the fire. Hassan closed his eyes and listened. The storm was dying at last. The rain had almost stopped, though gusts of wind occasionally rocked the house, the last vestiges of a storm that had raged too long.

Elena rested easily in his arms, cuddling against him. Making love to her had been a mistake, he knew, the result of too many days spent wanting her and knowing he could not, *should* not, have her. But at the moment it didn't feel like a mistake, not at all. If not for his purpose for coming to Texas, he would think loving Elena was more right than anything he'd ever done.

To dig into her grief now would be wrong in the same way. An emotional connection would complicate matters. And when this was over he didn't want Elena to think he had used her. He was a man who would do whatever was necessary to accomplish his goal...but not that. Never that.

Who was he kidding? The emotional connection was already there. It had been almost from the beginning.

"How did Johnny die?" he asked softly.

Elena shuddered and pressed her body more closely to his. "He was murdered," she whispered.

Hassan closed his eyes for a moment, feeling Elena's pain for such a violent loss. "What happened?"

"It was my fault," Elena said, tears in her voice. "We were going to stay at home and watch TV, but I changed my mind and decided I wanted to go to the movie. I just...I'm never impulsive, and I wasn't then, but...but there was nothing on television and I decided we should go see the late movie. But neither of us had any cash. I jumped in

insisted. I keep it at work, just to pacify him." She shook her head gently. "I could never shoot it."

Hassan had not met Yusuf Rahman. Since he himself had taken an American bride, Elena's mother, perhaps he was more modernized than the Arab fathers Hassan knew. Still... "What did your father think of your plans to marry Johnny?"

"We never told him. We were going to, but...but I knew he wouldn't approve, so we postponed the inevitable."

"And after Johnny was killed?"

"I told my father, then. I had to. He kept...trying to marry me off to his friends or their sons, and I would have none of it. I wasn't ready. I didn't think I would ever be *ready.*"

"And now?" Hassan whispered.

"I was so certain I didn't need anything but my work to have a good life," she confessed. "It's my fault Johnny was killed, I sent him to that ATM. His death...it hurt too much. I didn't want to go through that, ever again." She lifted her hand and caressed his cheek. "But you...you make me realize that my life is empty, in so many ways. Maybe I've lived safe long enough."

He captured her wrist and brought her palm to his mouth for a quick kiss. "You can't blame yourself for what happened," he whispered.

"How can I not?"

He did not want to think of Elena with another man, loving another man so much that she wanted to spend her life with him, sleep with him each night, bear his children. But she had grieved for too long. She needed someone to give her permission to stop punishing herself.

"Did he love you?" he asked, the question causing an unexpected pain.

"Yes," she whispered.

Hassan turned toward her bedroom. Already he wanted Elena again, and tonight...tonight he would not deny his passions or hers. Tomorrow would be soon enough to face reality.

He laid her in the bed and gently removed the blanket he had wrapped her in. The room was more dark than not, but since the rain had stopped and the clouds had been blown away, a hint of moonlight lit the room and Elena's bare body.

Tonight they were stranded. He couldn't call Rashid, he couldn't search Elena's computer. Tomorrow morning, the real world would intrude once again. Reality would impose itself upon them soon enough. Too soon.

Hassan joined Elena on the bed, lying beside her to kiss her throat, her shoulders, the pebbled nipples and the soft slope of her breasts. She reacted so intensely to every caress, to every flicker of his tongue. Her body grew warm, he felt her gentle quiver with his lips. As he took a nipple deep into his mouth and raked his palm up her thigh, she muttered something unintelligible, a word lost in throaty passion. She spoke again, and this time he heard her too clearly.

"Stop."

He did as she commanded, taking his mouth and his fingers from her body and propping his head in one hand to watch her. "Stop?"

He expected an argument of some kind, but instead was gifted with a wicked smile. Elena laid her palm against his chest and very tenderly pushed him onto his back. "This time," she whispered, "let me make love to you." She laid her mouth on his throat and kissed him there, gently, then not so gently. Her fingers teased his flat nipples for a minute or two before taking a winding trail down his body to rest on his hip. His hands did their own exploring, as Elena rained kisses over his throat, his jawline, beneath his ear,

It was almost night again, the sky growing gray. There were no clouds tonight, there would be no storm to drive her to Hassan and him to her. Too bad.

He parked his truck, rather than letting her out at the door, and she didn't argue when he left the driver's side and circled around to open her door for her. He smiled and offered his hand, and she took it. Hand in hand, they walked to the front entrance of her building.

The elevator ride up was slow, silent. Elena's heart pounded. At the door to her condo, Hassan hesitated and released her hand. "I really should call my brother tonight."

She nodded, understanding. "I'm sure your family didn't expect you to stay here this long."

"No," he said in a low voice.

"I have lots of work to do myself," she said absently, glancing up and down the long hallway. "You know, paperwork. Answering e-mail. That sort of thing."

"I wouldn't think of keeping you from your duties," Hassan said, his own eyes everywhere but on her.

"Good night," Elena said softly, and then she made the mistake of looking Hassan in the eye, just as he made the mistake of looking squarely at her. The emotions the simple eye contact roused were unexpected, but they shouldn't have been. She felt that gaze in her gut, in her weakening knees. In her heart.

"Of course," he said, a soft smile turning up the corners of his wicked mouth. "Rashid can wait."

Elena reached out and grabbed the front of Hassan's shirt and gave a gentle tug. "So can my paperwork."

He fell into the room, pushed the door closed behind him, and locked it, before taking her into his arms.

Elena buried her face against his shoulder. How could she want him, still? How could she ache for him?

Chapter 10

Elena practically ran down the hallway. She was late, but by no more than fifteen minutes. It was a miracle she was here at all. She'd overslept, the first pair of panty hose she'd put on had run, and Hassan had not wanted to let her leave. Wearing coveralls instead of her gray suit would have saved her at least ten minutes, but this was not a coveralls day.

She hadn't intended to take Hassan home with her last night, after a long Saturday at the ranch and a quiet Sunday ride home. They had said, more than once, that their affair was just for one night. It would be too complicated to expect anything more.

But when the time had come to say goodbye...they hadn't. She felt like a kid again. Just five more minutes, just one more time...the thought made her smile as she burst into the office.

Kitty's head snapped up.

"Are they waiting?"

Kitty nodded.

their own way, fulfill their own dreams. After Johnny's death, those dreams hadn't seemed so real, anymore. Had all her dreams died with him? She'd never looked at it that way before, but perhaps that was true. She'd given up, so easily.

Cade didn't approve of her working for her father. That was the obstacle that kept them from being close, the way a brother and sister should be. He always told her she could do better, and got angry when she did not agree.

Hassan made her realize that there was a world beyond Rahman Oil, a life waiting beyond her heartache and her determination. Had she settled for less than she should have? This weekend made her wonder.

Rashid had not been happy with Hassan's less than informative report, nor had he been pleased that the phone call came a day and a half late. If big brother knew that Hassan had actually slept with Elena, he would be furious and most likely order him home. But that was only one reason for not telling Rashid everything. His relationship with Elena was none of Rashid's business.

In order to impress Elena, he wore one of his best suits. In order to woo her, he carried a dozen perfect red roses. She'd told him to drop by her office in the afternoon, but he couldn't possibly wait another three or four hours. A smile flitted across his face. Elena Rahman, CEO, fearless lover, tender heart, was such an amazing woman. He had never known anyone like her.

He stepped into the outer office as Elena's door opened. For a moment he wondered if perhaps she sensed his presence. He had begun to think they were that close, that spiritually intimate.

But it was a man who stepped out of her office, and then another. Elena was in the midst of the crowd, and when she

Yusuf Rahman was *El-Malak*.

"I've been looking forward to meeting you, Mr. Rahman," Hassan said calmly.

The Brothers of Darkness despised the Royal family of Tamir, but Rahman's expression remained aloof, without emotion. "It's a pleasure. I hope my daughter has been accommodating during your visit."

Poor choice of words, given the timing, but Hassan did not react. "She's been most helpful," he said. This was the man he needed to get close to, this was the reason for his journey to Texas. If he were to find the prince, it would be through *El-Malak*. "But of course I have been hoping to meet with you personally. Elena seems quite knowledgeable about the business, but she is, of course, only a woman." He could not make himself glance her way. She would be furious, and rightly so.

Yusuf Rahman was not at all offended. As Hassan had suspected, *El-Malak* thought like an old-world Arab. Women were inferior, and should be subservient at all times.

"It would be my great pleasure to meet with you over dinner," Hassan said, nodding at Rahman. "Elena, too, of course," he added in an offhanded manner. "Leon's?"

It looked as if Rahman were about to refuse, and then reconsidered. "My house," he said. "Eight o'clock." He gave Elena a tight smile. "Just the three of us. I'm sure we can accomplish more in the privacy of my home than we would in a crowded restaurant."

"I would be delighted." Hassan finally made himself look at Elena. She was furious, her eyes hard as emeralds, her lips thin and her nostrils flaring slightly. Perhaps one day he would have the opportunity to explain to her that he had no choice but to play the game...if she would listen.

"Only a woman," Elena muttered, yanking off the jacket to her gray suit and tossing it over the back of her leather

calmly across the table from Hassan now that he had shown his true colors?

"I dread tonight," she said, shaking her head. "I can't believe Dad said yes! A few days ago he wanted me to talk to Hassan and then get rid of him. Why did he change his mind?"

"Money," Kitty said. She bent her head to smell the roses she still cradled in her hands. "In case you haven't noticed, your father has been a little obsessed with the subject, lately."

"I know. And we're doing so well."

"Yeah, but the assets are pretty tied up. There's not much liquid, at the moment."

"Enough," Elena said, sipping at the hot coffee.

Kitty snatched a vase from the closet, collected water for the roses, and arranged the flowers there on Elena's desk.

"Such a thoughtful gift," she said sweetly, her eyes on one particular rose. "Funny, but I don't recall any other business associates showing up with flowers and a come-hither grin. Your father has sent flowers on your birthday before, but never red roses. This…this is different."

"Mind your own business," Elena muttered halfheartedly.

"I always do," Kitty said with an innocent air.

"Ha!"

The roses perfectly arranged in the crystal vase, Kitty stepped back and admired them. "Tonight should be interesting."

"Interesting?"

Kitty smiled. "I would love to be a fly on the wall."

Elena sighed. Hassan had left with the others, that coward. She suspected he would not be by this afternoon, as he had originally planned. If he valued his life, he'd give her time to calm down before he showed his face here again.

been tossed unceremoniously onto her couch. No water. No vase. Not a word. She definitely had not invited him in.

But he couldn't apologize, not yet. Things were likely to get worse before they got better.

"Tell me about your father."

For a moment he thought she was going to ignore him. When she spoke, her voice was low. "My father is a very determined man. He knows what he wants and he goes after it with everything he's got."

"That is an admirable trait."

"Sometimes he goes too far," she added. "He will bowl over people as if they mean nothing, in order to get what he wants. I think he's that way because he grew up poor and made his own fortune. People who have to work for their wealth are sometimes deathly afraid of losing it. You wouldn't know about that," she added curtly.

"Neither would you."

She shrugged her shoulders. "True enough, but then what does that matter? I am, after all, only a woman."

Hassan sighed. "That did come out rather badly," he admitted. "I was only trying to..."

"Insult me?" she interrupted. "Drag me down? Humiliate me in front of the people I work with?"

"No." He muttered a curse beneath his breath. "Perhaps I was trying to impress your father."

"Well, you didn't impress me."

"Didn't you tell me that he would have the final say in whether or not a partner is invited into the business?"

"Yes, but..."

"And didn't you tell me that your father was an old-fashioned man?"

"Yes. What does that..."

"So if I want to stay, I need to find my way into his good graces. Do you not think that he might be more willing to

a woman, romance the socks off of her, tell her she's yours, make her..."

"No," he interrupted. "I have never, not once in my entire life, claimed a woman as *mine* the way I claim you now."

She tried to shake her head. "You are such a liar," she said softly.

"But not about this," he said, leaning toward Elena to give her a quick, deep kiss she did not turn away from. "Not about this."

wonderful, and there was a generous plateful of it on the table tonight.

Elena didn't eat many meals at her father's house. Their contact, always just a little bit strained, was confined to the office these days. They both seemed to be more comfortable with their professional relationship than their personal one.

Yusuf Rahman was a stern father, and in the past several years he spent less and less time at the Rahman Oil refinery. But he knew the business, and so did Hassan. The three of them talked business over lamb, cucumber salad and stuffed grape leaves.

Elena knew her father had no tender feelings for the Royal family of Tamir, but he hid his sentiments well tonight, and was gracious and cordial.

Even though he sat directly across the table from her, Elena didn't look at Hassan any more than she had to. The words he'd spoken when he'd pulled into the service station stayed with her. *My woman. Never before. Not about this.* That last statement was almost an admission of dishonesty, one she didn't care to dwell on, at the moment.

Hassan didn't look at her often, either. And the glances he cut in her direction were quick, almost furtive. There were times he seemed dismissive. Was this condescending attitude all for her father's sake?

When the meal was finished, Yusuf offered tea and cigarettes. Hassan accepted the offer of tea and passed on the cigarettes, thank goodness, as they made their way down the wide hallway to the study.

Like the rest of the house, Yusuf Rahman's study was perfectly ordered and suitably cold. His desk was massive, his chair and the sofa against one wall covered in the finest leather. The books on the bookshelf behind his desk were eclectic. There were industry manuals, of course, as well as

perhaps it was time to consider such a move. Her father viewed her as a disappointment. He had put her in this position because she was his daughter and would listen to his advice. Was she anything more than a hardworking figurehead?

"Are you actually considering allowing Mr. Kamal to buy into the company?" she asked. Her voice remained calm, but her heart jumped into her throat. At the moment, she didn't know if having Hassan around on a permanent basis was a good idea or not.

Yusuf grabbed a cigarette from his top desk drawer and lit it, taking a long drag and blowing out slowly. "I am considering the proposition."

"You said you would not do business with the royal family of Tamir," Elena said softly. "What changed your mind?"

"Two things." Her father smiled as he lowered himself to the chair behind the desk. "First of all, it is always best to have one's enemies where one can keep an eye on them. Secondly," he sighed. "Money. Cash money."

"I am not opposed to taking on a partner," she said, "but we are in good shape, financially. Why..."

"The Malounian National Trust is in need of funds," he snapped. "For new schools," he added with a wave of his hand. "I think it would be a great joke to take money from the Kamal family and send it directly to the Trust. If the price for such a joke is that Sheik Hassan makes the occasional appearance to play at being a partner, so be it."

"So you'll say yes."

He hesitated and took another long drag. "Not tonight. I want to think about it some more, perhaps ask Khalid and Akram what they think of the idea."

Elena glanced toward the closed door. Where was Has-

"No security guards?"

"There's a service that drives by frequently at night, but no full-time guard."

He mumbled a few indecipherable words beneath his breath, something harsh and foreign and most likely vile.

"All right," she said as they stepped into the elevator. "What's wrong?"

He glanced at the camera in the elevator. "Nothing."

"You're acting so..."

He silenced her with a kiss that was quick and deep and tasted of desperation. When she opened her mouth to finish her statement, Hassan kissed her again, more thoroughly this time. Something inside her melted. Her anger, maybe, her unwillingness to forgive.

When the elevator stopped at her floor, Hassan took her arm and led her into the hallway. He hovered over her protectively.

He didn't say good-night when they reached her door, but stood behind her while she unlocked the dead bolt with her key.

"You need coffee," he said as she stepped into her home.

"Your kind of coffee?" she asked. "I won't sleep at all if I drink so much as half a cup."

"All right," he said, leaning against the doorjamb. "*I* need coffee. My kind of coffee."

She couldn't make herself close the door in his face. "All right. The kitchen is yours."

He only glanced at the bouquet she had tossed on to the couch, and even though his jaw clenched he said nothing. As he headed for the kitchen, Elena collected the flowers from the couch. They were beautiful, she had to admit, and still fresh, thanks to the vials of water attached to each stem.

By the time she entered the kitchen, Hassan was already working on the Arabian coffee. She didn't say anything as

"I don't know what to think anymore. About this. About us."

"I am afraid that you will never forgive me," he whispered, reaching down to tuck a strand of hair behind her ear.

She gave him a small smile. "Kitty said I should, you know. She thinks you have potential." Her smile faded. "It's just that I've dealt with that *only a woman* crap all my life. I didn't expect it from you, even if you were just playing along to get on my father's good side."

He took a step closer, pressing his body to hers. "There are things about me you don't know."

Her entire body went cold and her heart dropped to her knees. "You're married."

"No!"

"Dying," she whispered.

He shook his head. "No. I'll tell you everything, when the time is right. Will you trust me until then?"

Elena Rahman didn't trust anyone, not completely. She lived on guard, she relied on no one but herself. She'd lived that way for so long, she wasn't sure she knew how to trust.

"Please," he whispered.

The need to trust was there, as strong and undeniable as Hassan's need to be trusted. "Yes."

Hassan's mouth covered hers, hungry and demanding, and she wrapped her arms around his neck and kissed him with everything she had to give.

She didn't know how much time they had left. If her father refused Hassan's offer, would the playboy sheik go looking for another refinery to invest in? A business far away from Evangeline? Of course he would.

Elena took her mouth from his, reluctantly and slowly. "Stay the night," she whispered.

"I can't."

was inside her, thick and fast and deep. She closed her eyes and held on tight. He pounded against and into her, fierce and uncontrolled. He drove deep, and she came fast and hard, crying out as her body shattered and trembled. On the waning waves of the intense response, Hassan climaxed with a shudder of his own, a growl and a throaty cry in husky Arabic.

For a moment they stood there joined and trembling, as their hearts tried to find a normal rhythm once again.

"What have you done to me, *hayati?*" Hassan asked as he slowly and gently placed her on her feet.

"*Hayati,*" she whispered. "What does that mean?"

"My love," he answered without hesitation, placing his palm on her cheek and resting his forehead against hers.

She smiled. "Stay the night," she said, for the second time.

The way he held her, the way he called her my love, she knew he wanted to stay. She knew he didn't want this night to end any more than she did. But he growled an answer.

"I can't."

The Rahman estate was dark, but there was a sophisticated security system protecting the house itself, and motion detector lights in the front yard that had come on as Hassan and Elena had left after their dinner with the old man. Hassan knew that if he tried to near the house now, as Rahman slept, he would trigger the alarms and the lights and he would learn nothing.

Dressed in black and stepping carefully, Hassan walked the perimeter of Yusuf Rahman's property, studying the house and looking for signs of security he had missed. Did *El-Malak* have an armed guard who kept a low profile?

As Hassan studied the house, his mind slipped back to Elena. What would she do when she discovered that her

Chapter 12

Confusion wasn't a condition Elena was accustomed to. When it came to business she knew exactly what she wanted and the way she wanted it done, and she was prepared for every contingency. Sometimes things went wrong; that was business as usual. Problems never bothered her, since she expected and was prepared for them.

But she'd been without a personal life for so long that she didn't know how to handle indecision in that area. She didn't know how to handle the battle going on in her heart. She certainly didn't know what to do with a man who made love to her like he couldn't ever get enough, and then walked away.

Hassan confused her. He wasn't the type of man she'd ever dreamed of being attracted to. Like it or not, he was too much like her father. Old world. Demanding. Too macho for his own good. But Hassan had something Yusuf Rahman did not: A good heart. She knew it, even when he infuriated her.

* * *

Hassan knew he couldn't break into Rahman's house without getting caught. Security was too tight. So he did the only thing he knew how to do. He got Rahman and his bodyguard/driver out of the house, and when he was certain *El-Malak* was well down the street, Hassan walked boldly to the front door. For the occasion, he had dressed in the high-necked silk jacket, shalwar, and turban of a Tamiri prince. His traditional costume was dark green and snow white, accented with a gold and emerald clasp and the air of authority befitting a sheik. He wasn't going to sneak into Rahman's domain, he was going to bulldoze his way through the front door.

As he had expected, Nawar answered, barely opening the door two inches.

"Mr. Rahman is not here," she said, her voice only slightly accented.

"I'm sorry I missed him," Hassan said, giving the housekeeper a wide smile. "Perhaps you can help me. It seems I misplaced an emerald ring, when I visited last night." He wiggled a bare left hand. "I have a nasty habit of twisting the ring and taking it off. I can't tell you how many times I've left it behind."

"I will look for your ring, Sheik Hassan," she said, just beginning to close the door in his face.

Hassan's smile faded. The woman was intimidated, by his size and his royal standing and the simple fact that he was a man. But Rahman had intimidated her more, apparently. She wasn't anxious to invite anyone into the house. "The ring is a family heirloom," he said before the door closed completely. "I need it. Now. I would like to look for it myself."

After a moment's hesitation, Nawar opened the door and stepped back. "Look quickly, please," she said as she

might easily be broken. How often did Rahman look at the box? How long before he knew it had been tampered with? Judging by the layer of dust on the box, his luck might hold out, this time. The dust also killed any hope that recent information might be found here, but the fact that it had been well hidden forced Hassan to continue. He unsheathed his knife and slipped the blade beneath the lid, popping the lock easily. He had no idea what he would find inside. More cash? Another map?

Hassan was momentarily disappointed when he opened the box to find it contained a brown leather wallet and nothing else. He removed the wallet from the box and flipped it open, only to find himself staring at the handsome face of a young blond man. John Edward Holmes, according to the driver's license.

Hassan's heart began to pound harder. This was Elena's Johnny. He flipped quickly through the wallet and found a photograph of Elena, young and smiling. There was also a photograph of the couple, cheek to cheek. The wallet contained forty-three dollars and some change, everything Johnny had been carrying that night.

El-Malak had killed Elena's fiancé, or else he'd had one of his men do the job and turn over the wallet as proof.

He heard soft footsteps in the hallway. Smoothly and briskly, he returned the wallet to the box and the box to its hiding place. He took the emerald ring from his pocket and rolled it beneath the desk. By the time Nawar opened the door, he was standing in the middle of the room, hands on his hips and an expression of dismay on his face.

"Did you find it?" he snapped.

"No." Nawar shook her head. "Perhaps you lost the ring elsewhere."

"It's here," he said. "Somewhere." Without moving from his place, he glanced around the room.

he loved her, and then leaving without a proper explanation. And now this. He'd never been late before.

Following a perfunctory knock, her office door flew open and Hassan, surprisingly clad in Tamiri dress, swept in with a grin on his face. His eyes found hers for a brief moment, and she had the oddest sensation that the smile he continued to wear was false. She couldn't put her finger on the reason, and when Hassan turned his attentions to her father, she dismissed her worry as fantasy. God, she had been so much better off when there was no man at all in her life. Hadn't she?

"My apologies," Hassan said, bowing slightly in Yusuf Rahman's direction. "I did not mean to keep you waiting."

Elena watched her father try to smile. It didn't quite work. "Quite all right," he said tightly. His eyes swept over the turban, silk jacket, and flowing pants. "Is this a special occasion?"

"I believe so," Hassan replied, his eyes remaining on the man who stood before the window. "We have business to discuss."

"I have come to no conclusions," Rahman said gruffly, obviously irritated. "It has only been a few hours since our dinner and discussion of your proposal. Did you think I would decide while I slept?" He narrowed one eye suspiciously.

The two men faced one another, Hassan almost a half foot taller, Rahman tense and about to lose his fleeting patience.

"Relations between your country and mine have been strained for quite some time," Hassan said softly, his smile gone.

"Yes, they have," Rahman agreed.

Hassan placed his hands behind his back. "The troubles have been going on for a long time, and are not of our doing.

She was so mad she trembled. She felt the quiver in her bones, and her face was hot. Surely she was beet red. All of a sudden, the whirlwind romance that had swept her off her feet seemed ugly. Corrupt, he had said. Hassan had seduced her so she'd agree to this...this travesty. Did he think she would be *flattered?* Did he think she wanted to marry some big, chauvinistic, sweet-talking Romeo? "If you two are going to talk about me as if I'm not present, do it in the conference room down the hall. I have work to do."

They turned and headed toward the door, surprisingly chummy.

"And Mr. Kamal," Elena said, trying to keep her voice calm. "You and my father can make all the plans you want, but I wouldn't marry you if you were the last man on earth."

At the doorway, they both turned to face her. "You're right," Hassan said, his eyes boring into hers. "She can be difficult." He smiled at her. Smiled! "But she is also very beautiful."

The two men left Elena's office before she could lay her hands on anything suitable for throwing at them.

Hassan knew he would likely never see Elena smile again. She was furious, and rightly so. But what else would make him insist on a face to face meeting with Rahman? It had to be something big, something shocking, something that would bring them together...and proposing marriage to Elena had come to his mind as the perfect solution.

Since it was Elena's father he needed to get close to, Rahman was the one to whom the proposal had been presented. Hassan had hoped the old man would be impressed by the traditional request to the father for his daughter's hand, and he had been. Elena had not.

He had also put himself in danger. Apparently Rahman

"No. She's at the refinery. Are those for her?"

"Yes."

"I'll take them."

Knowing what would happen, Hassan handed over the bouquet of mixed flowers.

"I have specific instructions on what to do with these, should you be so foolish as to show up bearing a lame peace offering," she said, opening the top drawer of her desk with one hand while taking the bouquet with the other. She drew a large pair of scissors from the drawer, and held the blooms over the garbage can as she began to cut. Petals were severed and fell atop the other discarded bouquet.

"I need to talk to her," Hassan said lowly, placing his hands on the desk and leaning forward.

"Good luck," Kitty said, returning to her computer and attacking the keyboard with a vengeance.

"You could help me."

Kitty quit typing and turned those steely eyes to him once again. "No, I've helped you enough. I've helped way too much, to be honest." For a moment her eyes softened, and she looked to be quite disappointed. "I thought you had potential."

"So I heard," Hassan grumbled.

"And then you turn out to be like…like…"

"Like who?" he urged.

Kitty clamped her mouth shut, refusing to continue. Of course she refused. Hassan knew what was to come next. *Just like Yusuf Rahman.* Just like Elena's father. If the woman wanted to keep her job, criticizing the company owner to someone who was just like him would not be wise.

"Tell Elena that I was here."

"Sure," Kitty agreed halfheartedly.

He couldn't say anything more, not yet. When this was over…maybe. If Elena would listen. If anyone would listen.

brought you, just as you instructed. They must've cost a small fortune.'' Kitty looked up. ''How did you know he would show up with flowers?''

''I knew because Sheik Hassan Kamal is a man who thinks he can do anything, and then buy his way out of it with a smile and a grand gesture.'' Elena wagged her fork at Kitty. ''He's probably never had to pay for his own mistakes, or answer for his own bullheadedness in his entire life.'' Her stomach was in knots. She couldn't eat, so when she quit pointing her fork at Kitty she lowered it to play with her spaghetti. ''You should have heard them,'' she added softly. ''They talked about me as if I weren't even in the room, as if I were…'' *Insignificant.* Her father had often made her feel that way, but she'd expected better of Hassan.

''Jerk,'' Kitty said enthusiastically. ''Domineering, conceited, dimwit.''

''I thought you liked him.''

''I do, kinda,'' Kitty confessed. ''But this is why you asked me over for dinner, right? So we can trash the guy and get him out of your system.''

''No,'' Elena said with a shake of her head. ''You're here to keep me from doing anything stupid.''

''Like what?''

''Like calling Hassan, or letting him in if he comes to the door.'' *You're here to stop me from listening to my heart and saying yes, no matter what.*

''Never fear,'' Kitty said. ''I will protect you.''

Elena continued to play with her spaghetti. Why was she so upset? She'd known all along that Hassan was too much like her father, with his inflexible, traditional ways and his domineering manner. She wasn't upset with him, she admitted silently, but with herself. She'd fallen for his sweet words hook, line and sinker. She'd allowed herself to feel in a way she'd never thought to feel again. No, she had

"Oh," Kitty said, picking at her garlic bread as the phone rang again.

Elena let the phone ring five times before she answered. Why had she switched off the answering machine? Oh yeah, she didn't want to hear what Hassan had to say. She didn't want those sweet, cajoling words recorded for posterity.

"Listen…" she said sharply.

"Elena, please."

It was the *please* that kept her from immediately hanging up again. Hassan was not a man to beg, to say please and thank you. And she did love the sound of his voice, traitorous as it was.

"Stop calling here," she said, hanging up quickly. Before she could so much as take a deep breath, the phone rang again.

Elena snatched the receiver off the wall. "Mr. Kamal," she said sharply.

"*Hayati,*" he whispered.

My love. Her heart leapt into her throat. "I can't believe you…"

"I can't explain," he said softly. "Not now, but one day, one day everything will be clear. Trust me."

"I can't," she said, turning her back on Kitty and resting her forehead against the wall, closing her eyes and trying to make her heartbeat slow. "I can't trust you." But she wanted to. She wanted, so much, to trust Hassan with her heart and her life.

The connection was severed, and Elena opened her eyes to see that Kitty stood there with her finger on the hook.

"Why am I here?" Kitty asked.

"To keep me from doing anything stupid."

"Exactly." Kitty took the phone from Elena, and when it rang again she answered. "Rahman residence." Her smile

* * *

Hassan quickly typed in the message, his eyes on the laptop screen. Nothing was completely safe, and he didn't trust e-mail at all, so he kept the message short and safe.

> Rashid,
> I have made some progress with Rahman, but this is a more tedious prospect than I expected. I need a few more days. Complications have arisen, but I have them well in hand. Will call on Wednesday, as planned.

He had to let Rashid believe there were no problems. Otherwise, big brother was likely to show up and ruin everything. He sent the e-mail, and then brought up a new message box. After staring at the blank form for a moment he typed in Elena's e-mail address. It was easy to remember. EJRahman at the company website. Did she check it herself? Or was that Kitty's job? If it was the secretary's job, Elena might never see this message. Still, he had to try. She wouldn't talk to him on the phone, she wouldn't speak to him in person…at least not yet.

> Elena,
> Give me a chance to explain. Wednesday night, 8:00, Leon's.
> P.S. Wear the red dress.

He wanted to see Elena now, but the extra day would serve two purposes. She would have a chance to calm down, and he could catch up on his sleep. Besides, he had an appointment with Yusuf Rahman tomorrow night. It was just as well that Elena not know of the meeting, since she would rightly assume that the subject would be her marital future.

Asking for Elena's hand in marriage had felt oddly right, even though it was a ploy, a way to get into *El-Malak*'s

playboy reputation, the man had a lot to learn about dealing with women. Well, she wasn't going to be the one to teach him!

The man was hopeless.

Before she got through the rest of her e-mail, Hassan's edict always in the back of her mind, her father stormed into her office. As always, a lit cigarette dangled from his hand. Elena suspected that was the real reason her father left the operation of the refinery to her. He couldn't smoke on site.

It was rare that he would make an appearance two days in a row. Even more unusual that both of those visits had been made alone, with only his driver, Salem, who waited with the car, accompanying him. Her father usually showed up with at least one of two of his pals in tow.

"Elena," he said, taking the chair on the opposite side of the desk and demanding her full attention. He waited until she had shut down her e-mail box before he continued. "I would like to speak to you about Sheik Hassan."

"I have nothing to say about Mr. Kamal," she said, her voice calm and just a little curt.

"You've thought all along that the merger was a good idea, have you not?"

"I didn't realize the partnership included being handed over on a silver platter. I didn't know becoming a good little wife would be part of the bargain." Her temper flared, and her voice was no longer calm. "This isn't Maloun, and we're not living in the nineteenth century. You can't make me a part of the deal."

Her father remained calm. "And if I insist?"

Elena shook her head. "How can you *insist?*"

"I have never asked sacrifices of you, Elena," he said, trying to make her feel guilty. "I have pampered you, indulged you, allowed you to become the Westernized woman

thought would make an acceptable husband.'' He sneered. ''An American.''

Elena's heart clenched. ''That has nothing to do with this...''

''He died,'' her father snapped. ''That marriage was not meant to be.''

Anger rose up in her. How dare he try to use that tragic moment in her life to control her! ''Johnny's death was a terrible accident. He was the victim of a violent crime, he was simply in the wrong place at the wrong time.''

''Was he?'' her father asked calmly. ''It is a shame, but it seems that violent crimes happen all the time. Anyone might be at the wrong place at the wrong time. A secretary. A sheik. A CEO.'' With that he rose to his feet. ''I have a meeting. Think over what I've said, Elena. I'll expect an answer soon.''

Elena sat numbly at her desk while her father left the office. She remained there for a few silent moments. Had her father just threatened her life? And Kitty's? And Hassan's? When she was sure he was gone, she rose from her seat and walked into the outer office, where Kitty sat typing numbers into the computer.

''Get Cade on the phone for me,'' Elena said softly, her eyes on the empty doorway and the hall beyond.

''Sure,'' Kitty said, swiveling around and snatching the phone from its cradle. She had found the number in the Rolodex and punched in three numbers when Elena stopped her.

''Never mind,'' she said softly. ''Maybe later.'' With that she returned to her office, closing the door behind her. What was wrong with her? Her imagination must be getting the best of her, thanks to not enough sleep and too much excitement in her usually tame personal life. Her father hadn't meant anything sinister by that final comment. He had just

Chapter 14

Tonight they met in Rahman's study without Elena present. Hassan had been a little nervous about returning to the Rahman estate, but Nawar remained wisely silent about his visit earlier in the day. She had done nothing more than cast one sideways glance his way. After that, she ignored him and performed her duties silently and quickly, spending no more time in the dining room or the study than was necessary.

Hassan had changed into an expensive suit, leaving his traditional clothing behind for this evening. Tonight's discussion of marriage was, after all, strictly business.

"Elena will come around," Rahman said as he leaned back in his leather chair. "She is stubborn, but she loves the company and will do what's best, no matter what the cost."

Hassan raised his eyebrows slightly, trying for a superior, condescending air. "I never imagined that she might consider marriage to me a great sacrifice. Most women would not."

ily, Hassan would no longer be needed. Would he meet a
fate similar to that of Elena's Johnny? A bullet in the back
of the head? Maybe a bomb in his truck or on a plane?
Perhaps a butcher's knife in the heart?

What had Johnny's assassin whispered before he pulled
the trigger? Perhaps the young man had known, in those
terrifying seconds before his death, that it was his beloved's
father who took his life. Had Rahman been the one to ex-
ecute Johnny? Or had he sent one of his men to do the deed?
They might never know, but Hassan suspected *El-Malak* had
seen to the chore himself.

Hassan no longer had any doubt that Elena was innocent.
If she were involved with the Brothers she'd be more com-
pliant where her father's demands were concerned. She
would be here now, making plans for a wedding. But she
wasn't here. She fought her father at every turn, and he had
seen the distaste in her eyes, heard the hurt in her voice.
No, she had no idea what her father did, what he had
planned for her future.

If she knew what kind of man her father really was, she
would not still be here, trying her best to please him.

No matter what happened in the days to come, he could
not leave Elena here. Not as long as *El-Malak* lived.

Elena had spent most of the day at the refinery, so she
stopped by the office still in her coveralls and steel-toed
shoes. Her hair was pulled back, out of her face, and she
wore no makeup. A smudge of grease, here and there,
marred her coveralls, her hands and her face.

It had been a long day, and it had started badly, since she
hadn't slept well last night. Her mind kept spinning, turning
this way and that as she tried to find rest.

And tonight...tonight Hassan expected her to show up at
Leon's for a romantic dinner. Let him wait. She had no

She set the single red rose down and dug into her purse, coming up with a hundred dollar bill. "Here," she said, handing it to the kid. "Take all these and what's in the van, and take them to the Evangeline Nursing Home. Make sure everyone gets something."

The hundred soothed the pain of hauling all the flowers out of here and making another stop. "Sure thing," he said, reaching for the white box.

Elena beat him to it. "Everything except this," she said.

Kitty shook her head and groaned, but an almost-smile touched her face. "You're going to do something stupid, aren't you?"

"Probably," Elena said, not at all distressed.

"Want me to tie you up until the urge passes?"

"No, thanks," Elena said, carrying the white box into her office.

"Good luck," Kitty mumbled.

"Thanks," Elena said as she closed the door behind her. "I'm going to need it."

He half expected her not to show up. When 8:00 arrived and there was no sign of Elena, Hassan almost left the restaurant. But he decided to give her fifteen more minutes. At 8:17, when she pulled into the parking lot, he was still there. Waiting. Waiting! Sheik Hassan Kamal never waited, for anyone or anything.

He watched her step out of the truck and give the keys to the valet. She hadn't worn the red dress, probably because he'd asked her to. But he had no complaints. The midnight blue dress she wore was very nice. Silk, he saw as she came closer. The dress hugged her body here and there, emphasizing her slender shape, the swell of her breasts and her hips. It was short enough, cut just above the knee, to give

into an intriguing dance. He saw the questions in her eyes. He could not answer, not tonight. Perhaps she knew that. "Then what will we talk about?"

"Oil refineries. Horses. My sisters. Kitty. Chocolate. The proper way to make coffee. Kahlil Gibran."

A slow, lazy grin broke across her beautiful face.

"And anything else that makes you smile that way."

Glancing into the rearview mirror, Elena saw the headlights on Hassan's truck as he followed her into the parking lot. He'd insisted on seeing her home, and she hadn't argued. Not much, anyway. The meal and conversation had been much more pleasant than she'd expected. She'd planned for war. A battle of epic proportions. An indignant assault on him for all his crimes.

And yet she'd had fun. Hassan definitely had more than his share of charm, and he was a great dancer. Dancing with him tonight had been different than the first time, because he knew her body and she knew his. They moved together too well, now. And she'd only known him a week. A week and a day.

She hadn't admitted it, and probably never would, but it had been that one sentence in his note with the rose that made her accept his invitation. *You know me better than anyone.* She felt the same way about him. In a matter of days, Hassan had worked his way under her skin in a way no one else ever had, and she didn't know how to shake him free. More importantly, she didn't know that she wanted to.

The arrogant jerk who had spoken to her father about marriage, excluding her from the conversation, was not the same man she had grown to love. She didn't understand why, or how, but she had no doubts. Which was the real Hassan? Had he manufactured the personality she had come

"What?" he asked, stepping onto the elevator to stand before her.

The doors closed once again, and the elevator began to move upward.

"Was everything you ever said and did a part of your plan to be a partner in Rahman Oil?"

"No," he answered sharply.

"Why should I believe you?"

The elevator stopped on her floor and Hassan moved aside, taking her arm as she stepped into the hallway. "Can't you believe me without question?"

"No," she said honestly. "I can't."

Hassan walked her to her door, thoughtfully silent as they took those last few steps that carried Elena home. She unlocked the door and turned, not ready to invite him in, not ready to send him away, either. He reached out and touched her face, gently tracing the line of her jaw with one finger.

"Blind faith," he whispered. "There comes a time in everyone's life when they must find it. When they must trust without reason, believe without proof. I've known you a week, no more than a blink of an eye in a lifetime, and yet I am asking you now to have blind faith in me."

"What if I'm incapable of...blind faith?" she asked, her heart pounding so hard she was sure it thudded louder than her voice.

"You are not incapable of such trust," Hassan said, lowering his head slowly, bringing his lips to hers. "You've simply never had need of it before."

He kissed her, wiping all thoughts of argument from her mind, stealing the last of her resolve with that sinful mouth. And that was all it took. One kiss, and she was ready to forget and forgive anything. His hand rested on her hip, warm and possessive, as he kissed her thoroughly.

Blind faith. More than anything, she wanted to be able to

an already hardened nipple. Sparks shot through her body, and when he took that nipple deeply into his mouth, the sparks turned to lightning that pooled between her thighs. He suckled tenderly, but not too tenderly, until she arched her back and her body cried for more. Instinctively, her thighs parted, and Hassan lifted his head to look down at her again.

Enough light spilled into the room from the hallway to illuminate his body and hers. She marveled at the sight of his flesh touching hers. His hard chest against her pale, soft breasts. His arms, corded with muscle, keeping his weight from her. His eyes, showing her nothing but passion, now. Any earlier indecision was gone, swept away by desire and need and blind faith.

She hooked one leg around his, entwining her body with his, bringing him closer. One anxious hand raked down his side, coming to rest on his hip. His body against hers, the feel of flesh to flesh and heart to heart, the rise and fall of his chest…every breath was arousing. Exciting. Most of all, she was filled with the certainty that this was *her* man, *her* lover. In the heart and soul she possessed him, and he possessed her.

The tip of his erection touched her where she throbbed for him, as he lowered his head to kiss her neck, to nibble and suck there until her body no longer cried for his. It screamed.

When he pushed inside her she arched her hips and closed her eyes, urging him deeper, letting herself get lost in pure sensation. Every stroke drove her closer to completion, every sway of his hips and hers was like another step in a dance toward the highest cliff. If there was danger, they didn't see it. They simply danced.

He surged deep, and with a cry Elena shattered. She dropped off the edge of the cliff, falling hard and fast. Has-

Last night she had asked for a translation of the words he'd spoken as he loved her, and he had refused. She hadn't pressed, which was good. He would have had to lie, if she insisted.

It was too soon to tell her that he had never felt this way about a woman. That he would die for her. That he loved her.

He was tempted, so tempted, to sweep Elena up, carry her to Tamir, and leave her there while he came back and tended to business. He wanted her safe, and as long as she lived in the circle of the Brothers, she was not safe. Unfortunately, Elena was not the kind of woman one swept up and carried off. She wouldn't stand for it. Would she?

She woke slowly, and lifted her head to smile at him. "Good morning."

He stroked a strand of hair away from her face. "Good morning."

"I'm glad you're still here," she whispered.

Did she think he would sneak out of the room while she slept? "So am I."

She settled down, cuddling against him. "Oh, I dread going to work today," she groaned.

"Then don't," he said, almost gruffly.

"I have to."

He didn't want Elena anywhere near Rahman Oil, not today, not tomorrow. If he could, he'd bundle her up this morning, take her to Tamir, and leave her in the only hands other than his own that he could trust.

"Why do you stay there?" he asked softly.

Elena rose up to look him in the eye. "What do you mean?"

"Why do you work for your father? He treats you badly, sometimes. He doesn't give you the power to make decisions." He felt a growing anger for her. "You're too good

Chapter 15

Hassan leaned against the phone booth, one hand holding the receiver to his ear, the other pinching the bridge of his nose. He'd come to the shopping mall to make his call, again. The background noise would make it difficult for anyone to listen in, even though he felt confident that no one was following him.

It was early evening in Tamir, and he took a chance that Rashid would be in his quarters and have access to his personal phone.

"I know I said I'd call last night," he said calmly, in answer to Rashid's testy admonition. "I was detained."

"By a woman?" Rashid snapped.

"Yes," Hassan answered.

Rashid had to be as careful as Hassan, in choosing his words. The security breach had everyone taking extra precautions. "When will you conclude your business?" he asked, no more anger in his voice.

"Soon."

office talking to Kitty. Not about business and not about Hassan, but about little things. Clothes. Preferred shades of lipstick and nail polish. Elena even asked Kitty if she'd ever read Kahlil Gibran.

She'd allowed a man, an aggravating, confusing, wonderful man to change her life. It was true that she barely knew Hassan Kamal, and yet she did trust him. Love him. Want him with every fiber of her being. Given what had happened in the past week, she should be skeptical, suspicious, wary...but her heart was light and full of unexpected joy.

Her good mood was spoiled by the arrival of her father and more than a half dozen of his cronies. Most of them she recognized. A few she did not, and that piqued her interest. The men, all well dressed in dark suits and wearing very serious expressions, stepped off the elevator and headed for the conference room. Her father and Arif trailed behind.

Elena stepped into the hallway. "What's going on?" she asked.

Her father turned to face her, and so did his companion. Arif, who was taller than Yusuf Rahman and much thinner, even smiled at her. The grin was tight and unfriendly, totally without warmth.

"It doesn't concern you," her father said sternly.

"How can that be?" she asked, puzzled and annoyed as she stepped down the hallway, closing the distance between herself and the two men. "I'm CEO of this company. Like it or not, everything that goes on here concerns me."

The old man glanced toward the conference room door at the end of the hallway.

"Elena, we will talk later."

She looked toward the conference room herself, and caught a pair of curious, strange eyes peering from the door-

He raised a hand to silence her. "Tonight I want you to keep him away from the refinery. I will have a guest there this evening, another potential investor, and I don't want the sheik around to get in the way."

All she could do was nod, as her father turned and stalked to the conference room, closing the door behind him with a resounding thud.

Elena stood there for a moment, alone in the hallway. Arif had just suggested that she marry Hassan and then...what? He would have an *accident?* Like the *other one?*

She turned around and headed for her office, shaking off Kitty's confused questions about what was up in the conference room. She closed the door behind her and went to her desk, sitting down easily and opening the bottom left drawer.

There, beneath a stack of papers, sat the weapon her father had given her, months after Johnny's murder. Johnny had been killed with a 9mm weapon. Was this...? She closed her eyes and shook her head. No. It couldn't be. No matter how cold and distant her father could be, he wouldn't...he couldn't...

Besides, Johnny's death hadn't been an accident. It had been a cold-blooded, senseless murder.

But she hadn't imagined the threat in Arif's words, and suddenly her father's turnaround where Hassan was concerned made sense. He hated the Tamiri royal family, she knew he did. He had objected to doing business with them from the beginning. Had he changed his mind because Hassan's offer of marriage would give him some kind of elevated stature? And was he willing to kill his new son-in-law once he had what he wanted?

Hassan knew something was wrong the moment Elena opened the door to her condo, in answer to his soft knock.

"I was caught up in the moment," she said, cutting him off before he could finish his sentence. "That's all it was."

He didn't believe her. Something was wrong, and he wanted, more than anything, for her to tell him what had happened. He wanted her to trust him enough to tell him what had frightened her. She'd seen or overheard something, and she was doing her best to get rid of him. Why? Was she protecting the father she loved so much? Did she know the truth about *El-Malak,* after all?

"Elena," he whispered, moving his mouth toward hers. *"Hayati."*

She let him kiss her. She even kissed him back, for one long moment. Did he taste dried tears on her lips? Did she give away too much with the hint of desperation in her kiss? Her lips stiffened and she moved her head to the side, breaking the contact of mouth to mouth.

"Tell me what's wrong," he whispered, tracing her jaw with his fingers.

"Nothing's wrong. It's just...over."

"No. Not like this," he insisted lowly.

"I'll...e-mail you," she said. "I saw the address on your business card."

She wasn't going to tell him anything. He would have done anything to protect her, to love her, and she was dismissing him this way because his presence was no longer convenient. "You'll *e-mail* me?" he asked, unable to hide his anger.

"Unless you'd rather I not," she said, again trying to be cool and distant.

Hassan stepped back. He didn't know what had happened, but he did know one thing. For some reason Elena had been forced to choose between her father and her lover, and she had chosen *El-Malak.*

purposes. Including using Hassan to ensure her silence, if he learned what she was up to.

She'd call Cade first, she imagined, and then the police. Her heart flipped over. Could she call the police on her own father? Could she report that she suspected him of murder? It would be simple enough to test the weapon in her desk drawer against the bullet that had killed Johnny, she imagined. Even after eight years, they would surely have all the evidence filed away somewhere.

Elena asked herself *why,* and then shook off the question. She knew why. She and Johnny had never told Yusuf Rahman that they were going to marry, but somehow he had found out. And he had disapproved, as she had known he would. Instead of telling her he knew of her plans and was not pleased, he'd taken care of the problem in a more permanent way. And then he'd held her hand at the funeral and let her cry on his shoulder. What kind of a man was he?

Something inside her had wanted, so desperately, to tell Hassan everything tonight, to lean on him and ask for his help. It wasn't a lack of trust that stopped her, it was the heart-clenching certainty that her father would kill Hassan without a second thought, if the sheik turned out to be more trouble than he was worth.

She had barely survived burying Johnny. Burying Hassan would kill her.

She jumped when the phone she was watching rang, and quickly snatched up the receiver.

"Elena," Kitty's agitated voice cracked. "Something's going on at the refinery."

Elena looked at her watch. "Why are you at work? It's almost nine."

"I was trying to finish up the payroll. I was almost done when I looked out the window and saw all these cars headed up the road toward the refinery. Maybe a dozen."

Chapter 16

The front door to the admin building was unlocked, and all was quiet. Elena took the elevator, fidgeting as it rose too slowly. When the doors opened she rushed into the hallway and ran to her office. Again, the door was unlocked, and as she surveyed the scene around her she found she couldn't breathe. Kitty's chair had been knocked onto its side, and most of the papers that had been sitting on her desk had been swept to the floor.

Elena lifted her eyes to the window. At the moment, everything looked normal at the refinery. She'd always thought the plain, functional plant became beautiful at night, when the lights came on and it was made brilliant against the black sky.

Beautiful or not, at the moment something was wrong. She ran into her office, her first instinct taking her to the bottom left drawer of her desk. She lifted the papers that hid her gun and stared at it for a long moment.

Johnny might well have been killed with this very

lieve that Elena would trust him enough to ask for his help. He didn't.

Hassan ran into Elena's office and opened the drawer where he had seen the weapon her father had given her. He half expected to see that it was gone, that Elena had taken the Heckler & Koch with her, but the pistol sat there, untouched. Without hesitation, Hassan took the weapon and checked to make sure it was still fully loaded. It was.

As he went to the window, he jammed the weapon into the waistband at his spine. In the parking low below, Elena stood beside her truck, still as a statue as she stared toward the refinery down the road. His own truck was parked at the back of the building, situated among a row of maintenance trucks. If Elena looked for it, she would find it. If not, she would have no way of knowing that he was here.

Instead of jumping in her truck, she turned her back on the office building and started walking. Not down the street, but through the wooded area along the side of the road.

She was sneaking up on the refinery, rather than approaching dead on. Why? He didn't like any of the answers that came to him, as he ran for the stairs.

Elena stopped at the east gate, found the proper key, and unlocked the padlock. So far, everything looked fine. Oh, God, if Kitty wasn't here she had no idea where to look. She didn't dare call the police, not with the threat of death hanging over Kitty's head.

She stayed in the shadows as she walked toward the main area of the refinery. It was up and running, pumps thumping, steam whooshing. From here, everything looked fine. She walked the edge of the property, looking for signs of trouble. There were so many half-empty warehouses, so many places to hide...

And then she saw movement at the water treatment build-

fittings. She took another step and saw her father, who had been concealed behind a large pump. He held a gun trained on someone. Kitty? And he was flanked on either side by men armed with automatic rifles like the one Salem had been carrying. Imraan and Noori both worked here, in the water treatment building.

She took another step, and saw that her father threatened not Kitty, but a bound and gagged man she immediately recognized. Prince Lucas Sebastiani. The missing crown prince of Montebello. But…how? Why? Elena didn't have time to unravel the reasons the prince might be here as she studied him. He appeared to be unhurt, but was gagged and lashed to a water pipe that ran from floor to ceiling.

''You'll bring a nice ransom,'' her father said to the prince. ''A ransom which will help to rebuild the Brothers of Darkness.''

Gagged as he was, Prince Lucas couldn't respond, but the look he gave Yusuf Rahman was anything but frightened.

''Dad?'' Elena said, stepping into the light. Imraan swung his weapon toward her.

Her father waved Imraan off, and the weapon ceased to be a threat to Elena. Her eyes remained on her father's face—a harsh, unrepentant face.

''What is this?''

''What are you doing here?'' he responded.

''Is Kitty here?''

He sighed. ''Yes. She's unhurt and will remain unhurt as long as all goes well.'' His dark eyes latched onto her face. ''You do like her, don't you?''

Why did she suddenly feel that saying yes would put Kitty's life in danger? ''She's a good secretary.''

The man who was her father, a man she didn't know at all, looked at her and knew she lied. She knew it by the

a thud from outside. Something loud that was capable of penetrating the concrete walls and the water above.

Her father waved his weapon toward the corridor. "Noori, find out what that was." After a moment, he sent the other man, also, ordering him to report back quickly.

With his guards gone, he took special care to train his weapon on the prince.

"And now?" Elena asked, edging closer.

"We will hold the prince for ransom, and with the money we receive for his safe return we will rebuild the organization."

"And what about me?" she asked. "I know everything. You killed Johnny, you've been using this refinery as a...a front for your organization. How many people have you killed?" she whispered. Then she shook her head. "Never mind. I don't want to know."

"Nothing will change," her father insisted. "You are my daughter, and you will say nothing."

"And if I do?"

"Everyone you know will pay for your mistake," he said coldly. "Kitty. The old couple at your ranch. Cade Gallagher."

Her blood ran cold and again her knees wobbled. It was an effort to stay on her feet. She had a strong urge to fall to her knees, cradle her head in her hands, and pray for this nightmare to end. But it wasn't a nightmare. It was real. Too real.

"Where is Noori?" he asked, glancing toward the corridor he could not see well from his vantage point. "He should be back by now."

Again a noise intruded, and this time it was easily identifiable. Gunfire. A moment later, they heard the noise again. She saw the panic on her father's face, the anger at his

but she did not move away from the prince. She couldn't. She had too many sins to atone for. How many deaths had she unwittingly been a part of?

A shot rang out, but there was no pain. Nothing. She opened her eyes and watched as her father crumpled to the ground. The prince she shielded looked up and so did she, just as Hassan, gun in hand, swung over the catwalk hand-rail and dropped to the floor.

He went directly to *El-Malak,* who lay dying, and kicked the gun away from his hand. The man still breathed, but not for long, and he was in obvious pain. Hassan felt no sympathy for a man who would shoot his own daughter.

The terrorist opened his eyes and looked at Hassan. "He said you would be no trouble, that you were only interested in…the refinery," he whispered hoarsely.

"He? Who told you this?" The security breach, the man who had leaked the information that the prince was still alive and a renewed search had been instigated.

"I should've killed you the minute you…" It was all the wounded man could manage, and with another labored breath, *El-Malak* died.

All hell broke loose, armed men rushing into the room, more armed men on the catwalk above. Elena ran to him, throwing her arms around his waist, shielding him as she had bravely, and foolishly, shielded Prince Lucas. With one look around him he realized why. The small army that had arrived, clearly identified by their windbreakers as FBI, thought he was one of the terrorists. In a nonthreatening gesture, he lifted his hands, and the gun, into the air.

Two men worked quickly to release the prince, who immediately cleared up the confusion. "No," Lucas said sharply. "He's one of us." As his bonds were cut he

that my memory would never come back. A few months ago I saw my face on the television. In the story they mentioned Montebello, and that was all it took. My memory started to come back, a piece at a time. I took to the road, for a while, not wanting to bring the chaos and confusion of my life to those who had been kind to me." He looked away, as if he didn't want to say more.

"Months ago?"

The prince nodded. "It's been a confusing time, and my memory has only recently been completely repaired. I contacted an old friend, who's with the FBI. They had learned that a possible kidnap plot was in the works, so I agreed to be the bait. I haven't even had time to call my father and let him know I'm alive."

"Your return to Montebello will be most welcomed," Hassan said.

The prince cocked his head, and a new, thoughtful light twinkled in his eyes. "Return with me. What a great show of unity that would be. Who could say that Montebello and Tamir can't be allies after this?"

He couldn't deny the value in that idea. And that was, after all, why he had come to Texas.

"I must speak to Elena first."

The prince's smile came back. "She is yours?"

Hassan sighed. "I hope so."

Three FBI agents arrived to escort the prince to a waiting helicopter. "She's very brave," he said. "And very beautiful."

"And I just killed her father," Hassan muttered as they walked down the concrete corridor.

"Saving her life and mine in the process."

Hassan nodded. He wished he could be sure Elena would see it that way. Outside the water treatment building, chaos ruled. A helicopter waited, rotors whirring. Terrorists, sol-

threw her to the ground, his body landing on top of hers as the shots rang out.

When he lifted his head, he saw Arif's body lying just a few feet away, the terrorist's weapon laying on the ground near his limp hand. An FBI agent kicked the weapon away and checked for a pulse at Arif's neck. He found none.

Breathing fast, Elena rose to her feet with Hassan's assistance. He caught her to him and held on tight, shielding her from harm and the sight of the body on the ground. He led her away from the terrorist's body, holding her close as he searched for a place where they were not surrounded by betrayal and death. Against the building, partially shielded by a concrete wall support, he finally breathed deep.

"It's going to be all right," he said softly, stroking Elena's hair, taking great comfort from the feel of her silky hair, the warmth of her body.

She shook her head against his chest. "Nothing's going to be all right. Nothing. Kitty called me, and...I didn't know what to do. I tried to call you at the hotel," she said breathlessly. "You weren't there. I thought you'd left."

"I will never leave you," Hassan said, his hands lost in her hair. Now and forever, she was his to protect. His to hold.

"My father was a terrorist," Elena whispered. "He did terrible things. He...he killed Johnny."

"I know."

"He would have killed me, too, if..." her head lifted slowly. Her eyes met his, and very quickly went from soft and weepy to hard and suspicious. "You *know?*"

"We'll talk about it later," he said, laying a hand on her cheek. "There's no need for you to be scared, not ever again. I'll stay with you. We'll get married, we'll..."

"No, we won't," Elena said, her tears gone as she put the pieces of the puzzle together. "You *knew*. Of course

"Elena," he said as he backed away, raising his voice so she could hear him well. "Not every word was a lie. Not every moment was a part of the game. Have faith," he shouted.

She shook her head. Her voice was too low for him to hear but he read her lips.

I can't.

Hassan jumped onto the helicopter, and almost immediately it lifted off the ground.

"Is everything all right?" Prince Lucas asked.

Hassan kept his eyes on the ground, on a small figure in black coveralls. Her head was tipped back to watch the helicopter fly away. "Brave and beautiful," he said, loud enough for the prince to hear. When he could no longer see Elena he faced the prince. "And stubborn!" he shouted. "Incredibly, impossibly, stubborn!"

gry for Elena's sake. And would remain so for some time, it seemed. "Do you want to live there?"

"No," Elena said sharply. She had so much to make amends for. Maybe this was a good place to start. "I'll sell it," she said. "And with the money I'll start the...the Lydia Parker Trust." She smiled softly. That might be the first clearheaded idea she'd had in days. "I'll manage it myself," she said. "And this time I'll be damned sure the money goes for schools and food." One of the first things she'd learned, from the FBI agents who were still underfoot, was that the Malounian National Trust funded weapons, not Malounian women and children in need.

The refinery had not been shut down, but it was running on a skeleton crew. A good number of her Malounian employees had been long time members of the Brothers of Darkness. But not all. Thank goodness Umair had known nothing about Yusuf Rahman's activities. What would she have done without him these past two days?

Umair had been home asleep when the excitement had taken place. He'd been angry to hear what had happened, angrier when the FBI grilled him. But he'd come off clean as a whistle, and was busy doing his part to rebuild and restaff the refinery.

The decision about the trust made, Elena retreated to her office and closed the door. The door muffled the activity in the office, but didn't erase it completely. Since the rescue of Prince Lucas, the press had been hounding her for interviews. Yesterday had been an absolute media frenzy. Today things were calmer, but Kitty had the added duty of keeping persistent reporters out of Elena's office. She needed peace and quiet; she needed a few days at the ranch. And heaven help her, she didn't want to go there alone.

She sat at her desk and opened the top drawer. Sitting here, atop the odds and ends, was Hassan's business card.

"I did," she said softly. "Your secretary said you were out of town, and I didn't want to bother you..."

"You didn't want to bother me?" he interrupted. "Elena." He shook his head. "I came as soon as I heard."

Her lower lip trembled. She hadn't cried since Thursday night, and even then, her tears had been quick. Painless, compared to the ones that welled up in her now.

Cade groaned. "Oh, honey, don't cry." He protested, but still he wrapped his arms around her.

Elena let the tears flow, dampening Cade's shoulder, letting it all out. He murmured the kind of encouraging things a brother should, never once saying "I told you so." For that, she would love him forever.

When the tears were gone she lifted her head and looked up at him. "You were right all along," she said, sniffling.

"I wish I hadn't been," he said gruffly.

"He killed Johnny," she whispered, even though there was no one else around to hear her horrible secret. "And my mother." She started to shake, just a little.

"Dammit," Cade said angrily. "I should have dragged you out of here years ago."

He had tried, hadn't he? In subtle ways, with gentle prods instead of force, and yet...

Elena shook her head. "I wouldn't have gone."

"I know," Cade sighed.

"I was so determined to earn my father's trust and his love and his approval, and all this time..." she sniffled again, angry and hurt in a way she could not easily express. "What did you know that I didn't?" she asked. "What happened between you two?"

Cade patted her on the back, gently and consolingly.

"I'll tell you all about it one of these days. Soon. But not today. This is not the time or the place." He cursed low and profane. "He doesn't deserve your tears, Elena."

got to get out of here. You have the number, in case you need me.''

''Good idea,'' Kitty said gently. ''Cade going with you?''

Elena shook her head.

''Want some company?''

Yeah, but he's on the opposite side of the world. ''No,'' she said. ''I need some time alone.''

Kitty nodded. ''Umair and I will take care of things here.''

''I know you will.''

Kitty stopped what she was doing and gave Elena her full attention. ''Is he coming back?''

Elena shook her head and glanced over her shoulder to find that Cade listened intently for her answer.

''No,'' she finally whispered.

Hassan stood on the East Terrace, looking out at the familiar sea. The sounds of the ocean usually soothed him, but not tonight. He had not been anything near *soothed* for days. It was as if his brain was constantly spinning. His heart was in no better shape.

Prince Lucas's homecoming had been hailed as a miracle. His family and his country rejoiced; they rejoiced still. Hassan had been welcomed into the Montebellan Palace as a trusted ally, and as family. It was all he had hoped for, when he'd left for Texas, but he'd found himself unexpectantly humbled by a father's gratitude and a mother's tears.

He had hoped to find some peace here, in his home, with his family, but there was no peace to be had. Elena had sent him away, she had sworn she did not need him or anyone else. She refused to have faith.

Hassan didn't even hear Samira coming. One moment he was alone, the next his sister stood beside him, her own

"What difference does it..." he stopped mid sentence. True, neither of his suggestions for marriage could be called romantic. But circumstances had not allowed for anything so conventional as a bent-knee proposal. "I asked, she said no. The details are not important."

"I know you too well, Hassan," Samira said gently. "Instead of asking, you probably demanded that she marry you. In a very charming way, of course," she amended. "But still, I would imagine a woman might expect to be *asked,* in this day and age."

Hassan didn't have a response to that observation. Not one he would repeat to his little sister, in any case.

"But you did tell her that you love her, didn't you?" Samira pressed.

Hassan took a deep, calming breath. "She knows how I feel."

"How does she know?"

He had shown her, in every way he knew how. He had told her, once.

In a language she could not understand.

"You would like her," he said. "Elena is brave and beautiful and very, very stubborn."

"And when are you going back to Texas to collect her?" Samira asked with a smile.

"Elena said she needs time," he said. "After what she's been through, she can have all the time she needs."

Samira raised her eyebrows. "Knowing how patient you are, I have to wonder how long you think that might be."

Hassan grumbled at the sea. He was not going to stand here and sulk over what might have been if he'd approached the matter differently. He'd give Elena the time she'd requested, but his patience was not endless. "I would think a week to be plenty of time."

Samira laughed lightly and squeezed his hand.

messages into a new box, add a short note of her own, and hit the send key.

And honestly, after this she was going to swear off interfering in other people's lives. It was positively draining.

Hassan dragged out his laptop for the second time that day. He didn't normally bother to check it more than twice a week, but he kept hearing Elena's halfhearted promise. *I'll e-mail you.*

He didn't expect to find anything this morning, but a message came up on the screen with Elena's name attached. When he opened it, the note at the top was not from Elena; it was from Kitty.

> I found these in the trash. I know I should mind my own business, but I thought this was something you should see.
>
>   Kitty

A short distance down, he found three separate notes. They all touched him, they all made him anxious to get the next plane for Texas. Especially that last question. *Where the hell are you?*

He dressed, not in a suit or jeans or coveralls, but in a traditional costume. Dark blue and gold, for this occasion, including the turban and a sapphire ring. He made the journey down the hallway, his footsteps almost silent, soft Tamiri boots quiet on the tile floor.

The guard at his father's study door saw him coming and opened the massive door, bending at the waist as he admitted Hassan to Sheik Ahmed's office. The old man, who rarely saw his second son before noon, was obviously surprised. He put down the pen he had been signing papers with.

"Do you want me to beg?" he asked. "To show you the reverence I have never shown you before? Fine. I beg you for your consent. I have never asked you for anything. Never. I will never ask you for anything else."

The old sheik's expression softened as he rounded the desk. "Stand up," he ordered, fluttering his fingers. "I won't have my son on his knees."

Hassan didn't move. "Then give your consent."

"Why? You have never cared for my opinion or my approval before," Ahmed snapped. "Why now?"

Hassan lifted his head and met his father's dark gaze. He had never relied on his family; like Elena he had thought he needed no one in this world. "I cannot give Elena everything I want to give her alone. I must have you, Mother, Rashid, the girls…I must call on you all to give Elena what she needs."

"What does she need?"

If he went to Elena alone, without what he wanted most to give her, they would survive. They would love and thrive and grow. They would be happy. And still, he wanted, so much, to do this for her.

"She needs a family. The family her father took from her, from the day he murdered her mother to the day he died, standing there telling Elena that she meant nothing to him." A surge of anger welled up inside him. "She deserves better. And I can't give her everything she should have without your help."

The sheik's expression softened, his posture relaxed. "Do you love her so deeply?"

"Yes."

The old man shook his head while he motioned with his hand for Hassan to rise. "Stand up. If this woman means so much to you, you have my wholehearted support and my official and unofficial endorsement. When is the wedding?"

charming and handsome would easily fill his shoes. But in her heart she knew better. She loved him. She always would. And she didn't know if she'd ever see him again.

She closed her eyes. Blind faith. She understood the concept, she truly did, but it was hard to have faith in anything when her world was falling apart. The father she had worked so hard to love had been willing to kill her, in the name of his terrorist organization. Her mother hadn't died in a freak car accident, she'd been murdered by the man she'd loved and married, the father of her child. And Johnny...poor Johnny hadn't done anything wrong but to love the wrong woman.

The easiest thing to do would be to give up on love completely. But she didn't want to do that.

Elena wanted to love Hassan, and she wanted him here. She took a deep breath, reached deep inside herself and tried to find her faith. Faith that love could conquer all, faith that one day her prince would come.

And she found it, in a wave of peace and a certainty that everything really was going to be fine. She and Hassan would be together, somehow, some way. Some day.

The gray snickered, and Elena opened her eyes to glance behind her. Far away, it looked like someone was riding the black stallion. Impossible. No one but Hassan could ride that horse. She stood, shielding her eyes with her hand and squinting for a better look. Black and flowing white, that was her first impression. Black and white. Since the horse sped quickly toward her, it didn't take her long to see that it was, indeed, Hassan on the stallion's back. She held her breath, tears filled her eyes, and as Hassan came near she couldn't help but smile.

He dismounted with ease and came toward her. Last time Hassan had ridden out here he'd been dressed as a proper Texan should be dressed, in jeans and snakeskin boots and

"Elena, mar…" Hassan stopped suddenly, took a deep breath and began again. "*Will* you marry me?"

"You're a prince," she whispered. "I'm just…" *Faith.* She smiled. "Yes."

His grin was brilliant. "I hope you don't believe in long engagements," he said. "I don't."

She shook her head. "Neither do I."

"Good." He took her arm and led her to the crest of the hill, where they both sat to look down on the river. "My mother is already planning the wedding."

"You were confident I would say yes?" she teased.

"I had faith," he said, reaching inside the leather bag and drawing out a yellow gold and emerald ring. He took her left hand and placed it on her ring finger.

"Me, too," she whispered as Hassan brushed one fingertip against the perfectly fitted emerald ring, his hand so large and capable against hers. It was a hand made for holding. "It hasn't been easy, but…I'm learning. Thanks to you."

Hassan leaned into her and kissed her, a deep kiss to seal the bargain. Or perhaps he was simply as hungry for the taste of her as she was for the feel and taste of him.

"It is tradition," he said, drawing away and dropping his eyes to the ring on her finger, "to offer the bride *mahr*. A wedding gift."

"The ring is beautiful," she whispered.

"There's more," he reached into the bag and pulled out a handful of pearls and emeralds. A bracelet, earrings, necklaces, another ring.

"Hassan, this is too much," she said as he dumped the pile of gems into her lap. They looked ridiculous against her worn jeans, out of place even as they sparkled in the sunlight.

"No," he protested. "This simple gift is not too much. I can never give you too much."

her finger, tracing the lines of his mouth as she did so. When her hand rested on his cheek she moved her mouth unerringly toward his. "I love you, too."

*   *   *   *   *

Next month, come to Elena and Hassan's wedding, where you'll see Cade Gallagher fall under the spell of beautiful Princess Leila in VIRGIN SEDUCTION by Kathleen Creighton, as ROMANCING THE CROWN *continues—only from Silhouette Intimate Moments!*

Here is a sneak preview of VIRGIN SEDUCTION...

Chapter 1

Leila almost lost her courage. The tall figure silhouetted against the evening sky and framed by gold-washed pillars seemed so forbidding, utterly unapproachable, like a sentinel guarding the gates of Heaven. But, oh, she thought as her heartbeat pattered deliriously in her throat, how commanding he looked in his evening clothes—how elegant, even regal.

Almost...almost, she turned to run away, to leave him there with his solitude. For uncounted moments she hovered, balanced like a bird on a swaying branch, balanced, she was even in that moment aware, between two futures for herself...two very different paths. One path was familiar to her, its destination dismally certain; the other was a complete unknown, veiled in darkness, and she had no way of knowing whether it might lead her to the freedom she so desired...or disaster.

She hovered, her heart beating faster...harder...and then, somehow, she was moving forward again, moving toward

He turned toward her and leaned an elbow on the balustrade.

When had she come to be standing so close to him? The sea breeze carried her scent to him...sweet and faintly spicy. The word *exotic* came to his mind. But then, everything about her was exotic. Was that why she seemed so exciting to him? The fact that she was different from every woman he'd ever met?

Don't even think about it. She's absolutely off-limits.

Or was it simply that she was forbidden fruit? Off-limits. Inaccessible. Except that, at this moment, at least, he knew that she was entirely accessible...to him.

And to think like that was insane. And insanely dangerous. He was dealing with a tiger out of her cage, nothing less.

Except that she didn't look much like a tiger at the moment, or anything even remotely dangerous. She looked soft and warm and sweet, more like ripe summer than forbidden fruit. Torchlight touched off golden sparks in the ornaments in her hair and in her eyes. Gazing into them, he felt again the peculiar sensation of not-quite-dizziness, as if his world, his center of gravity, had tilted off-center. Clutching for something commonplace and familiar, he took a quick, desperate puff of his all-but-forgotten cheroot.

Her whisper came like an extension of the breeze...or his own sigh. For one brief moment he wasn't certain whether it was her voice he was hearing, or merely the echoes of his own thoughts.

''Do you want to kiss me, Mr. Gallagher?''

Cade almost swallowed his cigar. *Do you want to kiss me?*

What on God's green earth could he say to that? Jolted cruelly back to reality, his mind whirred like a computer through countless impossibilities, distilled finally down to wonder whether his might even be the first lips to ever have touched hers, and the thought both excited and shamed him. Is that what it's all about? he wondered. Is *that* why I want her so much? Nothing to do with exotic beauty and forbidden fruit, only the thirst of the conqueror for undefiled lands to claim as his own.

His thirst was in danger of blossoming into fullblown lust.

He felt the flutterings of instinctive resistance; if only he hadn't! If only she'd responded openly, brazenly to his kiss, he might have been able to keep it as he'd intended it to be—blatantly mocking—and end it there. But that tiny faltering, that faint gasp of virginal hesitation... It stirred some primitive masculine response deep within him, so that her hesitation affected him not as a warning, but as a challenge. And an embrace meant only to lighten the mood and diffuse dangerous emotions became instead a seduction.

Instead of releasing her, his fingers stroked sensuous circles over the tightened muscles in her back and waist... Instead of pulling away from her he gently absorbed her lips' quiverings and delicately soothed them with the warmth of his own mouth. And felt her relax...melt into his embrace...as he'd somehow known she would.

He shifted her slightly, to a more comfortable, more natural position, and felt her body align with his as if it had been custom made for that purpose, a soft and supple warmth. He lightly sipped her wine-scented m... ed for the then discovered—too late—that he was every fiber of unique flavors of her, that he craved h... inside his brain. his being.

Tiny lightbursts of warning... God-knew-where Reserves of strength sum... mouth from hers—for made it possible for him... sound like the moaning a moment, no more... face in the graceful curve of wind in old trees

her racing pulse. Swamped with dizziness, afraid she might fall, she clung with desperate fingers to the arms that held her and fearfully opened her eyes. Eyes stared down into hers…eyes that burned with a golden gleam…eyes that burned her soul like fire.

"What—" She meant to whisper, but it was a tiny squeak, like the mew of a kitten.

His voice was so ragged she could hardly understand him. "Princess—I'm sorry. I can't do this. I can't…"

When she felt his arms shift, depriving her of their support, she gasped and caught at his sleeves. His fingers bit into the flesh of her arms as, grim-faced, he held her away from him, then with great care stood her upright and steadied her like a precariously balanced statue. Once more his eyes lashed across her, and she flinched as though from the sting of a whip.

"Dammit," he fiercely muttered, and then, as he turned, added with soft regret, "Another time, maybe…another place."

And he was gone.

Left alone, Leila stood where she was, trembling, hardly daring to move, until the scrape of footsteps on stone had been swallowed up in the shushing of waves and the whisper of wind.

Foolish…foolish… The whispers mocked her. Serves you right. This is what happens to pushy women.

But…what *had* happened, exactly?

Hugging herself, Leila whirled to face the glittering indigo vastness of sky and sea. She was shivering still, no longer with shock, but a strange, fierce *excitement.* Cade Gallagher had kissed her! Kissed her in a way she was quite certain no man should ever kiss a woman who was not his wife.

And that she had allowed it…? Fear and guilt added

ANN MAJOR
CHRISTINE RIMMER
BEVERLY BARTON

cordially invite you to attend the year's most exclusive party at the **LONE STAR COUNTRY CLUB!**

Meet three very different young women who'll discover that wishes *can* come true!

LONE STAR COUNTRY CLUB:
The Debutantes

Lone Star Country Club: Where Texas society reigns supreme—and appearances are *everything*.

Available in May at your favorite retail outlet, only from Silhouette.

Visit Silhouette at www.eHarlequin.com

PSLSCCTD

*Silhouette presents an exciting
new continuity series:*

When a royal family rolls out the red carpet for love, power and deception, will their lives change forever?

The saga begins in April 2002 with:

The Princess Is Pregnant!

by Laurie Paige (SE #1459)

**May: THE PRINCESS AND THE DUKE by Allison Leigh
(SE #1465)**

**June: ROYAL PROTOCOL by Christine Flynn
(SE #1471)**

Be sure to catch all nine Crown and Glory stories: the first three appear in
Silhouette Special Edition, the next three continue in Silhouette Romance
and the saga concludes with three books in Silhouette Desire.

And be sure not to miss more royal stories,
from Silhouette Intimate Moments'

Romancing
the Crown,

running January through December.